Four New Messages

FOUR NEW MESSAGES

Joshua Cohen

Graywolf Press

"Emission" appeared in the *Paris Review;* "McDonald's" appeared in *Triple Canopy;* "The College Borough" appeared in *Harper's Magazine;* and excerpts from "Sent" appeared in *Denver Quarterly* and *BOMB*.

This publication is made possible in part by a grant provided by the Minnesota State Arts Board, through an appropriation by the Minnesota State Legislature from the Minnesota general fund and its arts and cultural heritage fund with money from the vote of the people of Minnesota on November 4, 2008, and a grant from the Wells Fargo Foundation Minnesota. Significant support has also been provided by the National Endowment for the Arts; Target; the McKnight Foundation; and other generous contributions from foundations, corporations, and individuals.

To these organizations and individuals we offer our heartfelt thanks.

Published by Graywolf Press
250 Third Avenue North, Suite 600
Minneapolis, Minnesota 55401

www.graywolfpress.org

Published in the United States of America

ISBN 978-1-55597-618-7

2 4 6 8 9 7 5 3 1
First Graywolf Printing, 2012

Library of Congress Control Number: 2012936219

Cover design: Alvaro Villanueva

Emission   3

McDonald's   53

The College Borough   85

Sent   117

Four New Messages

EMISSION

This isn't that classic conceit where you tell a story about someone and it's really just a story about yourself.

My story is pretty simple:

About two years after being graduated from college with a degree in unemployment—my thesis was on Metaphor— I'd moved from New York to Berlin to work as a writer, though perhaps that's not right because nobody in Berlin *works*. I'm not going to get into why that is here. This isn't history, isn't an episode on the History Channel.

Take a pen, write this on a paper scrap, then when you're near a computer, search:

www.visitberlin.de

Alternately, you could just keep clicking your finger on that address until this very page wears out—until you've wiped the ink away and accessed nothing.

However, my being a writer of fiction was itself just a fiction and because I couldn't finish a novel and because nobody was paying me to live the blank boring novel that was my life, I was giving up.

After a year in Berlin, with my German language skills nonexistent, I was going back home. Not home but back to New York, I was going to business school. An M.B.A. It was time to grow up because life is short and even brevity costs. My uncle told me that, and it was his being diagnosed with a boutique sarcoma that—forget it.

Yesterday by close of business was the first time my portfolio ever reached seven figures, so if every author needs an occasion, let this be mine. Sitting in an office when I should be out celebrating my first million—instead remembering these events of five years ago to my keyboard, my screen.

But as I've said this is not about me—no one wants to hear how I'm currently leveraged or about my investments in the privatization of hospitals in China.

I met Mono—I'll always think of him as Mono—only once, a week before I left Neukölln forever. Left the leafy lindens and sluggish Spree, the breakfasts of sausages and cheeses and breads that stretched like communist boulevards into late afternoon, the stretch denim legs of the artist girls pedaling home from their studios on paintspattered single speeds, the syrupy strong coffees the Kurdish diaspora made by midnight at my corner café and its resident narcoleptic who'd roll tomorrow's cigarettes for me, ten smokes for two euros.

I was at a Biergarten, outside on its patio overlooking the water. The patio was abundant with greens: softly flowing ferns, flowers in pails, miniature trees packed into buckets to cut down on the breeze from the brackish canal. It was summer, still the evenings sometimes blew cool. Not this one. This evening was stifling. A few punks, scuzzy but happy, sat mohawked, barechested, feeding decomposing mice to their domesticated ermine. I was about to follow suit, had my shirt halfway up my beergut when he sat down—just when the sun was coming down.

Prose descriptions are safer than photographs (pics) and movies (vids). No one would ever identify the hero of a novel, if he'd come to life, solely by his author's description. Let's face it: Raskolnikov—"his face was pale and distorted, and a bitter, wrathful, and malignant smile was on his lips"—is not being stopped on the street.

Across from me Mono sat reading that novel, in English of course. And English led to English—he asked what beer was I drinking, an Erdinger Dunkel, and ordered the same.

To make conversation I said, Too bad we're being served by the Russian. The Turk—turning my eye to the eye of her hairy navel—is way hotter.

This is not to my credit. To his he just smiled.

It was a tight smile, lips chewing teeth, as if he wasn't sure how fresh his breath was.

I don't know why Mono made such an impression on my premillionaire self—maybe because when you're young and life's a mess, the world is too: young and messy. It could also have been the beer, hopped on malt, its own head turning my head to foam.

I was in my mid 20s, actually in that latter portion of my 20s, spiraling, like how a jetliner crashes, toward 30.

But Mono was young.

He had his decade in front of him.

We covered 30: scary, scary.

Also we discovered we were both from Jersey—me from south, he from central, but still.

Why here?

It was important to deliver this offhand. All expats worry about coming off spoiled or ludicrous, insane.

Why I came here was to write a book, I offered, which isn't working out.

He brought his mouth to his beer, not the other way around. The beard was still growing in.

He swallowed, said, Achtung, and as the sun disappeared told me this story.

Back in Jersey—this was only two months before the time of his telling but anything Jersey felt like years ago, amenitized among diners and turnpikes—Mono was a deliverer.

Like a priest, delivering from sin?

Or a recent arrival from Fujian with the fried rice, the scooter?

No, what Mono brought were drugs.

Drugs paid well but only for those actually supplying. Mono merely supplied the supply. This was not *the ideas economy*—whatever was supposed to save our country once we'd stopped physically making anything of value.

This was effort, was pick up, drop off, keep all names out of it and deal exclusively in cash. (*FYI,* Benjamin Franklin is one of only two people featured on bills never to have been US President.)

Mono worked for a man—and he was a man with multiple children and women and not a lost lanky kid like Mono—who called himself Methyl O'Nine (as in cocaine, benzoylmethylecgonine, also zero and nine were the last two digits of his retired pager).

He was a short, slim but muscled, comparatively black man with a ritually dyed henna fleck of a goatee discreet beneath voluminous dreads like plumbing gone awry.

Mono spent weekends moving his product.

Methyl was a hushed seclusive type—not just careful but temperamentally dervish in his sandals and gangsta hoodies—and never wanted his deliverers to know where he lived or with whom he supplied and so he'd meet Mono as he'd meet all the others who did Mono's job, on discrepant dim corners in Trenton.

Whenever he called Mono went and Mono went wherever Mono was called, which meant a lot of driving the Ford from near campus to fields and wharves and the parkinglots of midpriced restaurants.

Ford: bad brakes, transmission with the shakes, used to be his mother's.

Campus: a fancy private university approximately an hour south of New York.

Methyl's customers were mostly students—the idle rich, studiously clubby douches and athletic fratters, the occasional slumming neo-Marxist—but there were also the professors both adjunct and tenured. Some needed the drugs to write the papers, others needed the drugs to grade the papers, all needed the drugs—which they'd snort from atop the papers with rolled paper bills.

The students lived in student housing, the faculty lived in faculty housing (most student and faculty housing was identical), but Mono lived just outside Princeton—sorry, my mistake—in a collapsing bleachers of an apartment complex tenanted exclusively by the lowest paid support staff: the sad diabetics who mopped up the home game vomiting and this one security guard who protected the academics on weekdays but on weekends was regularly arrested in spousal disputes.

Mono hated being thought of as a dealer, as a danger. No respect for his opinion, no regard for his mind. And so he'd intimate deadlines, make allusions to debt, often just outright say it.

Enrolled but in another department.

Grothdyck? I snoozed through his seminar last spring.

I'm not sure if any of the students believed him, though I'm not sure what reason they'd have not to believe him and anyway it wasn't exactly a contradiction to be both enrolled and an impostor, a fine student and seriously druggish, deluded.

Mono's father had taught mathematics at the university—he'd made major advances in knotted polynomials, applied them to engineer a tamperproof model for voting by computer—and so was sure his son's application would be accepted, despite the crappy grades.

But it wasn't, it was rejected.

When he finally sold the house and moved away to chair the math department of a school in California—this was about six months before Mono and I sat together over beers in Berlin—Mono decided to remain.

Mono's mother had died—an aneurysm after a routine jog, a clean body in a bloodless bath—three years before these events. Her death was why his father had wanted to move, though Mono thought his failure to have been admitted to school had an influence—his father's professional humiliation (Mono was a professional at humiliating his father).

And the car his mother left behind precipitated Mono's fight with his father—when the professor began dating a former student or began publicly dating her. She'd brought the largest veggie stix 'n' dip platter to the gathering after the funeral.

She was also from Yerevan—super young and super skinny and tall with curly red hair curled around a crucifix that oscillated between the antennal nipples of her breasts—and as long as we're confusing ourselves with chronology, she was just two years older than Mono.

His mother's ailing Ford became his because his father already had a convertible.

Then one afternoon his father asked, Could you lend Aline your car for the day? She wishes to consolidate her life before the moving.

Mono said he said nothing.

His father tried again, Could you drive her yourself, to assist with the boxes?

Mono explained:

That was his father's way of telling him that Aline was coming to Cali.

My mother's car? Mono finally asked.

But you can forget about Aline. She's pregnant with Mono's half brother in Palo Alto and this is her last appearance.

At the time Mono's name was not yet Mono. That name was as new as Berlin.

Like *monolingual,* he'd said when we shook hands (his hand was sweaty).

Whereas the surname he'd been given was much more distinctively foreign. Not that he was supposed to divulge that name to his customers—to them, until he ruined himself, he was only *Dick.*

To get him to loiter outside your dorm or stand around licking fingers to count bills on the rickety porch of an off-campus sorority, you dialed Methyl, who'd say, He be calling a minute before he shows. Name of Dick.

Dick would usually show up within a half hour and though he was supposed to only get paid and leave, he never followed Methyl's instructions.

Instead he'd play older brother, stacking used plastic cups, making troughs of new ice, holding class presidents steady upsidedown for kegstands, reveling in free drinks and ambient vagina until recalled to work with a vibrating msg: NW6, say (Trenton's North Ward location six, where he'd make the night's next pickup—Methyl didn't trust anyone out with more than three deliveries at a time).

Dick stayed out later the later in the night he was called and so on a 3 AM delivery to a party that had run out that a colleague, *Rex,* had delivered earlier that evening, a party pumping for six or seven hours already through music playlists both popularly appropriate and someone's stepdad's collection of Dylan bootlegs and whose mixer juices and tonics had been exhausted, *Dick* would not be moved, especially not when a girl—the same girl who'd called Methyl, who'd told his deliverer to expect a female customer—threw arms around him and said:

They sent *you* this time!

Dick, who prided himself on remembering all his customers, couldn't be sure whether this girl, Em, was pretending to remember him or just wasted—and this should have been his first warning.

The couch, the absorbent couch, furniture in appearance like a corkscrew coil of shit—brown cushions, black backing worn shiny—soaking in the boozy spill and smoke of years, intaking fumes and fluids through the spongy membrane of its upholstery. They sat there, he and this girl who knew him only as *Dick*—this townie fake gownie and though he didn't know it yet the daughter of a Midwestern appliances manufacturer who maintained, this daughter did, upward of thirty anonymous weblogs: *Stuff to Cook When You're Hungover, Movies I Recently Saw About Niggers, My Big Gay Milkshake Diary, The Corey News* (which warned of the depredations of child stardom), *What I've Heard About Bathrooms in North America*—all irregularly updated but all updated.

They sat doing lines—is that my line? that's your line? this line's mine—and all was weightlessly intimate until Em turned to him and said:

This is from yours right?

Dick didn't answer immediately so she asked again.

This is on you?

Dick said, Sure.

Sure?

Whatever. We'll figure it out.

Em said, No not whatever. No figuring. Say it for me!

He felt like he had to stop himself from peeling her lips off her face as if they were price stickers, like they were designer labels as she said again:

Say it for me! This is your supply.

He said, This is *your supply*.

Em smiled.

OK, this is my shit. This shit is mine.

And she laughed and said, Dick! I'm so glad they sent you!

And he said, Actually only people who work for me call me Dick. My name's really Rich.

Rich?

Richard.

Rich hard what?

I'd show you my license, if I had it.

He'd been craving this opportunity to brag.

I was jumped last month in Philly, rival dealers, took my narcotics and wallet (a lie: he'd been drugfree on his way to a bartending job interview, the muggers barely pubescent, three kids as stubby as their switchblades).

You don't carry ID?

He reached into a pocket, found his passport, passed it around.

Em flipped through it, Did you enjoy Mexico?

I went with my parents.

You were an ugly child.

Discussions were: over changing the music and so changing the mood, about what band was good or bad in which years and with which personnel—is playing the bass harder than it looks? does a true leadsinger have any business playing guitar?

Anyway what kind of person would say which—*personnel* as opposed to *lineup*? *leadsinger* as opposed to *frontman*?

Is this coke cut? is all coke cut? and how is that not the same as *lacing*?

What innocents they were, *Dick* thought—the purity was theirs, not the drug's.

This one guy said, There was this girl I used to go out with who was the transitional girlfriend of a kid who starred in like every fucking movie.

Who was it? the party wanted to know, what every fucking movie was he in?

The guy told them.

Famous right? crazy crazy famous? Girls saved his face into screensavers, produced ringtones out of his voice. She was with him for three months off and on. Then I was with her and after our third or fourth date we had sex and you know what she said to me after?

What?

She said: *Peter, before you having sex was just like staring at the ceiling.*

Like what?

Again: *like staring at the ceiling.*

And that night that coital praise became an inside joke, like, whatchacallit, a party trope.

When someone went to the kitchen, opened the fridge, and retrieved another beer for you it was, Before you drinking beer was just like staring at the ceiling, when someone tapped out a thick fat line for you with their parents' Platinum Plus Visa card on the glass slab tiered above the baize bottom of the house's threequartersize poker table it was, Before you coke was just like staring at the ceiling, then that prefatory endearment was dropped with the tense and it was only, This couch is just like staring at the ceiling, This floor is just like staring at the ceiling, This ceiling's just like staring at the ceiling.

You had to be there but you're lucky you weren't.

Somebody left to buy the ingredients to bake a pie, somebody left to buy a pie, somebody left.

Cakes v. pies were debated, cupcakes v. muffins were too, the salient differences between them, the identities of the world's greatest lacrosse players were discussed, various names proposed both at the college level and pro. Pressing questions asked and answered: What's more degrading, working as a stripper or working as a maid? What's the best position to have re: Iran—preemptive strikes or sanctions inevitably targeting women and children? What's the best sexual position for virginity loss—for a man, for a woman, for a child? Is there a future for campaign finance reform after the veritable abortion of *Citizens United v. FEC*? If you could repeal any amendment to the Constitution, which (no one allowed anymore to pick the first ten, whichever amendment repealed Prohibition, or the thirteenth, fourteenth, or fifteenth)? If you were a fart, what type (how wet, what smell)? Ten Most Mortifying Moments? Most egregious party foul? If you could describe your entire life in only one word to only one dead grandparent, which grandparent and what word?

Etc.

Mono's apartment had been advertised as a one bedroom but having remitted the deposit he admitted to himself, why not, it was a studio. What the realtor maintained made it a one bedroom was a small little nothing nook by the door so minuscule that whenever Mono wanted to open the door he had to move the television onto the bed. His TV slept better than he did. The door's peephole had been blackened for a robbery. The window opposite gave onto parkinglot, he never kept it open, gas. On the floor, lotto stubs, scratchers he'd scratch with teeth. Underlabeled whiskey under the label. Flies at the bottom of a liter of cola. In the bathroom clothing hung from the showerhead smelling alternately feculent and moldy. The sink was mustached with shavings. He'd been using takeout napkins as toiletpaper for a month. The sounds he'd hear by morning were those of mice the size of his pinky sprayed newborn from the walls or, once, the whining die of the smokedetector's batteries. The apartment had no light because the bulbs had burnt out and he never remembered to replace them. Anyway Mono was rarely home at night and the television was enough light and the computer was sufficient too.

Mono was ISO work. He was perpetually interviewing and applying himself to applications because what's life for a man in the middle?

Interrupting binges where if you didn't have what they wanted you yourself weren't wanted.

Only feared.

Meeting people furtively but trying to be kind. Yet having that kindness misinterpreted.

I don't care what you think about the Yankees' outfield, one kid said, I just want my fucking drugs.

Yankee wants his fucking drugs? Mono unsure of what to say.

The kid apologized.

Accidental, his initial involvement. Mono had begun delivering when he began owing Methyl money—short one night on an eightball he was supposed to have split before a food court coworker bailed (that one week Mono worked at Quaker Mall).

He knew he had to get out when this past New Year's down the shore at a condo shuttered for the season a fierce former valedictorian who'd strolled with him along the snowy beach had said, Let's continue this conversation some other time—a convo about renewable energy—like when I'm sober and you're not my dealer.

Mono had had sex with her lesbian friend that night: she was stretchmark mangled, solicitous. She'd feigned abandon, collapsed on the bed, but just when Mono wanted to fall asleep she went to the bathroom to brush teeth, which was tender. The next morning she picked his jeans up from the floor and turned the pantlegs rightside out while Mono repositioned the pair of athletic socks in his jacket's breast-pocket—an advertisement for his packing a gun. That was the only time he'd had sex this year.

The résumé he'd been sending around he'd falsified: his experience including six months as executive assistant in a film production company he'd created, a year as a consultant to a pharmaceutical consulting firm for whose HR hotline he gave his own phone, figuring he could talk drug distribution with the best—while his other references tended toward the suspiciously familial: his cousin who'd developed a dating website and was too lazy busy getting laid to pick up the phone, another cousin who did the ordering for but did not own as Mono had stated Trenton's North Triangle Liquors—though when it came to education he demurred: granting himself only a B.A. if cum laude, supplemented vainly by a Dean's Award in English.

Despite this, he'd become inured to rejection: Never called back by that Suburban Poverty Task Force that needed someone with a liberal arts background to disorganize their archives, bend paperclips into helicopters and swans. Refused by that talent management agency requiring a front office rep. (he was overqualified, they qualified). A limousine driver, a limo dispatcher (ditto). Each being the juniormost position each business offered.

Monday punctually at noon the phone rang and Mono answered and a voice said, Mr. Monomian (the pronunciation was passable), I'm calling from Skilling Militainment Solutions.

Mr. Skilling, Mono said.

There is no Skilling. This is O. J. Muggs, recruiter, ret. capt. Marines.

Mono, sitting up in bed, said, Sir.

I'm afraid we can't offer you the position.

You can't? The position? But I haven't even been interviewed.

You won't be. This does not constitute an interview. Please say yes, indicating your understanding.

No I don't understand.

Don't fool yourself, son. Not even civilians are exempt from civility. Security isn't just armed convoys, it's also a sound reputation.

What's unsound about my reputation?

What you do in private is your business, until it becomes public, and then it's your employer's business, especially if your employer's employed by the government of the United States. War's all about image—and effective chaplaincy and counterinsurgency.

Come again?

You need to clear your profile, son.

My profile, what about it?

Your presence, you need to clean your presence.

I'm not following, and Mono canvassed his apartment, wondering whether the man had a camera focused on him or was just intuitive.

The internet, Muggs said, are you aware of your internet?

Mono was not aware of his internet. He'd never made a habit of googling himself—it was too depressing a venture.

Previously his life had passed undetected by bots. His life too modest for hits, too meek for the concerns of blog-postings and tweets.

Mono had always taken such paucity personally—virtual presence being, to him, presence nonetheless.

Whenever he searched there were only two results, two matches found: the first listing his name along with others of his class from Princeton High, the second aggregating what had to be all the names of all Jersey high school graduates ever to redirect them to wealth management services and medical tourism sites.

But now still abed, after ending the phoncecall, tugging his computer close and keying in *monomian*—typeable with two fingers, every letter but one kept to the right of the keyboard—he found a third.

The blog was called *Emission*.

The link was that optimistic bright blue that after Mono clicked would turn to the drab abused and nameless color of vomit.

The post's heading, Richard Monomian.

Mono withheld his vomit.

He scrolled to the end and the post was signed with that single name, *Em*, timestamped midday the day before.

But just as he was about to read the whole post from the top his computer emitted a pop—his father was messaging him over chat:

Greetings Diran!

That was Mono's birthname, before Richard.

Why are you not returning my calls?

Mono messaged:

cant talk now dad, then deleted.

Mono messaged:

its rich dad, then deleted again.

His father messaged:

Diran it is my hope you are not ignoring me.

Mono clicked the chatbox shut, blocked his father from chatting.

He read on:

Friday night @ party with RICHARD MONOMIAN. *He brought 'snax.'*

Wink! wink!

Thats what he does for a living. He brings snax that are OK priced but also of crackhead quality.

Anyways.

Were all just hanging out smoking getting our drink on telling stories about former bfs and gfs when RICHARD MONOMIAN *tells us this story.*

About another party he went to.

A high school party.

Now when the guy who brings the snax begins doing the snax and telling stories about high school you know its time to bag for home but for some reason we didnt.

This was spring break, end of senior year.

Before P'ton, obvs.

It was a big houseparty at a big house with the hosts parents away—remember those?

It ended with everyone oblitermerated passed out on random beds in random rooms and RICHARD MONOMIAN *searching around for an empty bedroom to crash in.*

And he found like a guestroom or spare for using the computer or phone in room and there was a bed in the corner or like a foldout sofa.

A girl was sleeping.

RICHARD MONOMIAN *said he didnt remember her name but even if he had remembered it and told me I wouldnt repeat it, thats not my style.*

RICHARD MONOMIAN *said this sleeping girl was cute, I guess not cute enough to rape.*

Instead he pulled his pants down below his ass tits and pulled down his underwear also.

RICHARD MONOMIAN grabbed his penis and stroked—he stood over her and stroked it!!

Dick fisting his shit! Dick fisting his shit!

Dick grabbed his hard dick hard and below him the girl kept sleeping.

He was on MDMA I think.

I think ecstasy and weeds.

Highlarious!

Suddenly he came: RICHARD MONOMIAN *blew a load that landed in her hand.*

RICHARD MONOMIAN *said he didnt wipe it up because he didnt want to wake her, he just pulled up his underwear and pulled up his pants and fell downstairs and out the door for home.*

Thats it.

All the deets I have.

Retardedly I didnt take a pic of him last night and cant find a pic online but Im sure one of my readers can and if you can then fwd: because I sometimes need a pic to look at to get less horny, Subject line: because I sometimes need a pic to look at to get less horny,

(And if youre that girl who woke one morning on a strange sofabed in a strange house with a jizzy palm worried about what happened, maybe you ran out to get tested, maybe you ran out to get the pill—this is it, youre welcome, be careful where you fall asleep, sista.)

At least his pic wasn't available. That was the best benefit of his previous anonymity.

Mono tried to remember what pics of him were around. Not many, few digitized. School portraits, a few snaps with friends moved away to colleges, and family poses, most of which his father had storaged. Easier to imagine a picture of yourself than to imagine yourself. He thought, why is it so hard to remember colors? And did anyone else think of death while being shot for an employee ID? (Besides the passport the only photo of himself he had was just that, from that week pretzeling at Quaker Mall.)

He stayed in bed, blowing through what cash he had left ordering to his door medium pizzas and Asian noodle decoctions waiting for Methyl to call with his next assignment as the legitimate world with its legitimate rewards stopped calling, stopped responding to his calls—him sitting up in bed, with the pillow verticalized between his legs as stuffed buffer between computer and any Monomians to come, searching himself, researching his name, "within quotes."

Three results went to four when another blog he suspected this Em of hosting linked to the *Emission,* then four upticked to six when two readers of those blogs linked up from blogs of their own.

Sometimes it was just an embed singly described, *Disgusting,* other times it was a capsule blurb that transclused: *Em, a college girl from Jerzee who's been keeping a party diary, writes about a guy masturbating on top of a sleeping girl . . . NSFW.*

But that was a particularly responsible example and most of the keywords were rather: *Wrong, Sinister, This is just totally scrotally insane.*

People thinking this funny precisely because it was legend, social lore—it didn't happen to them:

next time sleep with an umbrella
next time my girls not in the mood im gonna give her a monomian cumbrella lol!
wear rubbers!!

Within a week a hundredplus results all replicated his name as if each letter of it (those voluble, oragenital *o*s) were a mirror for a stranger's snorting—reflecting everywhere the nostrils of New York, Los Angeles, Reykjavík, Seoul, as thousands cut this tale for bulk and laced with detail, tapped it into lines, and his name became a tag for abject failure, for deviant, for skank.

To pull a Monomian.

To go Monomian.

Fucking Monomial.

No one, had you asked them, would have thought he was real. Only he knew he was real. And he only knew that, he thought, by his suffering.

Mono was on the internet all day but did not masturbate. Porn sites went unvisited. He'd type in half their addresses then stop and delete, hating himself because the computer couldn't hate him instead. The nonjudgmental nature of technology, if technology could have a nature—that struck him as unfair.

He restrained himself from leaving comments on Em's blog or from responding in any way by starting to blog himself because already people were posting under his name, were posting *as him:* Richard_Monomian, Rich_Monomian, Dickhardmon, Monoaturbator69, each claiming to be "the real meatspace Monomian."

IRL I jerked in my own hand then inseminated her preggers (wrote Modick).

Actually the bitch was so passed out I gave her an anal alarm-clock (wrote Dicknass).

The more the commenters commented, the more accurate even their inaccuracies felt, the more their elaborations felt essential.

The weekend after losing out on a janitorial job then failing to obtain two other minimumwage positions (jeggings folder, organic waiter), Mono began searching for something else, not for this proliferating porno about himself but for a number of basic variations: "how to get something off the internet," "how to remove stuff from the net," "slander on the web," "info on online defamation and how to fight it," "how to destroy a website entirely forever," "is destroying a website technically legal if the work is contracted to someone in another country," "how to knock out someone's server if you don't know anything whatsoever about hacking or even what servers are."

He found a forum dedicated to cybersecurity that counseled a girl whose exboyfriend had uploaded a sex vid to contact a lawyer and sue for removal plus compensation.

One chatroom included a comment from a genuine lawyer—"A Verified User"—advising a man whose wife had put up a website accusing him of being a compulsive gambler and not paying child support to contact him, he'd send a Cease & Desist for cheap.

That must have worked because the link www.my exhusbandrandyisalyingdegenerateteenfuckinggambler whosbadinbedanddoesnotpayforhisonlychildsfoodand medication.com was no longer functional.

Also the lawyer advised him to pay his child support: Buddy, that's just Christian.

Mono searched for lawyers in his area by typing "lawyers in my area." The number one result was a website called "What Is a Good Web Site to Find Lawyers in My Area." Like digging a hole to find a buried shovel to use to dig a grave.

Then Mono typed in "how to get people to take down libel from online," adding the local zipcodes.

At the bottom of the first page of results, the tenth hit, was a link to a digital paralegal.

That's what the header said, Da Digital Paralegal.

Mono didn't hesitate, his connections did: B4UGO Network

gave two bars, Chuck's Den gave three, Sally Sally Wireless Home—finally full strength.

He arrived at a site either terribly lowtech or trying to keep the lowest of profiles: a page all blank white like paper with only a single address centered, the contact, *dp@dadigital paralegal.com,* not even clickable—it had to be typed into the To: line of an email.

What Mono sent this address was tentative, vaguely worded: *Hello, my name is Richard and I am inquiring after your services,* and though it was very late at night—though these were his normal working hours, beginning around midnight when, if Methyl had called, he'd be commuting the speed limit down U.S. 1 South between campus and the stripjoints of Trenton—the DP wrote him back within the minute, before he had the chance to signoff, amid a last reloaded scan of the news:

Climate change was being called a sort of temperature socialism—it redistributed warmth to the colder months. This winter had set records. A woman gave birth to triplets, her twin to quintuplets. The father of all—the nondescript fertility doctor.

Elections don't end wars.

The DP's email, terse:

U still up—just call me, then it gave her number. Her name, appearing not as a signature by dully fonted macro but as if by regular typing, was *Majorie.*

Hello, *Majorie?*

No reason she'd let it ring ten times.

Yes, the voice lidless, up, what time is it?

You asked me to call.

No I know. I'm aware of my email.

This is Dick.

Dick who?

Reluctance then because he'd have to say it anyway, Richard Monomian, and then he spelled it out.

It's good to meet you M-O-N-O-M-I-A-N.

Behind her voice he could hear a toilet flush.

How does this work?

You were rather unclear in your initial query. But let me tell you to start, investing in taxi medallions is 100% safe and legal—a burgeoning business. I myself own ten I've leased at absurdly favorable terms.

You've lost me.

I have a comprehensive information packet if you'll only give me your mailman address.

My mailman's address? I'm calling about the internet.

A pause and then, *mailman's address* is just a code, of course—if you were active in the Celebrity Privacy movement you'd have answered *my mailman has no address,* then we'd be talking business. I take it you're no technophile.

No I'm a courier.

A courier. Is that your only problem?

Now after the toilet a sink ran. Majorie might've been washing her hands. Which Mono chose to take as the mark of a professional.

And you're a paralegal?

In the interests of disclosure I'm a paraparalegal. It's the same difference pretty much.

And where are you located? Could I come by your offices and talk?

Majorie gave a cough or burp, an unforthcoming eruction.

Excuse me, she said, I'm out of state.

Don't you realize we have the same area code?

I prefer to do business over the phone.

Why?

Security.

Are you recording this?

It's a federal law that you have to tell someone when you're recording their conversation.

Are you telling me that you're recording our conversation?

No.

Mono suspecting now that her office was her residence, which was a disaster, had to be. He heard—suspected he heard—junkfood wrappers crunch under slipper as she stalked around, as if testing the echoes of a floor's worth of partially furnished rooms in an old drafty inherited house: from the reverberant bathroom she, they, seemed to be now in a larger room or long hallway.

She told Mono she could help him, she did this type of freelance all the time.

Her voice was backed by clacking keys or particularly strident cicadas.

Do what?

First I customize a letter for your situation then I email it to the webmaster or mistress of the originating offending URL—that's uniform resource locator.

What does this letter say?

It's your standard-issue unequivocal demand: remove the original post from both website and cache and post instead a short retraction.

Saying?

This post has been removed. Or would you prefer a public apology?

I think the less said about it the better.

Then I'll ask the webmistress to sign her name to another email acknowledging the site falsified its information before sending that around to every linking site asking them to likewise take down content and threatening suit if they refuse to comply.

Every linking site?

Tell me this: Is what Em wrote true? Did you really spray all over that girl?

Mono, stymied, asked, We can't be sure that Em's her real name, can we?

Doesn't matter.

How long is this going to take?

There's no guarantee—the web's like sweaty footwear: stuff lives in there forever.

Mono imagined the smell of her slippers—sweat: ammoniac, uriniferous, vinegar, chipotle sauce.

How much do you need?

I won't accept payment in narcotics.

Could you get started tonight?

I'll get started the moment you transfer $1000. Paypal to my email.

I'm on it.

Don't worry, she laughed, I won't fall asleep on the job, and only the next morning did he realize she was making a joke about him splooging all over women in their somnolence, which wasn't funny.

hey kidderoos guess what Mama got today?

Re: that salacious stroking tidbit of earlier last week? . . . Just a note, below, after the jump.

Toward week's end the *Emission* posted not any scripted retraction but a screenshot of the retraction request itself, accompanied by Em's commentary:

This type of coercion has no legal basis whatsoever, Im not even prelaw and I know this.

So let me make this as clear as clear as clear can be, which on the internet MEANS CAPS:

I WILL NOT PUB A RETRACTION, Online Fidelity Fixers or whatever your ridongculous company is called that has no history anywhere, I dont think has ever been incorporated or registered or you get what Im saying and certainly has never filed taxes in the State of New Jersey [this hyperlinked to a state taxation page that said, "terms: 'Online Fidelity Fixers': No Record(s) Found"].

This story Richard Monomian told me is TRUE. He knows it is TRUE.

That he knows it is TRUE and nothing but the TRUE is why he hired you, Online Fidelity Fixers.

I looked you up globally, suckers!

What have you ever done? Your website hasnt been updated in two years [hyperlink to website]*!*

Who designed it, a retardy chimpanzee [hyperlink to vid of chimp, unclear as to whether retarded but still slurping its own feces]*?*

This email of yours is just a smear of yours truly. Funded by a desperate assaulter of women named Richard Monomian.

Who is also a dealer!

Whose coke is also BAD!

And you Mrs. J. K. M. Jorie, LA—l.egal a.ssistant requires an abbreviation, are you queerious?

This is amateur hour, yo.

By that later Thursday afternoon, the last waning work hours when bored deskbounds log on and comment to do anything but improve their own existences, tidy the file chains, or disburden the inbox, this post had racked up over 350 responses like:

MunchieZ: right on girl!

anonymous: u tell it!

anonymous: I am a practicing lawyer in the city and you Em are correctamundo as always.

jd: Im with u. I call bullshit.

m@jd: Bullshit!

bullshit: Bullshit! (first!)

anonymous: this letter is not even worth the paper it is not printed on.

(*Hugger89* and *go_deep* like that comment.

That comment had a comment—*see one reply:* monomaniacal wtf!?)

Friday morning after googling himself and finding that post Mono called Majorie and got a voicemail that said: You've reached Broken Wings: Last-Minute Frequent-Flyer Miles Broker to the Bereaved.

He waited for the beep, Call me. This is unbereavable.

He lay back in bed perusing a magazine he'd found weathered wet and unsubscribed to in the hallway last week, read from the cover in a whisper—*revista feminina*—as if a foreign language had the power to save him from what he did understand (was the internet as virulent in Spanish or Italian, in German or French?).

He flipped the pages, past the makeup styles and recipe tips—what Mexicans had the kitchens for this? had the flatware, stemware, and jobless hours?—heading into an article headlined *¿qué es la depilación láser?*

Mono wondered if he'd ever be able to masturbate again. Not above a sleeping stranger and not even to the internet, which had been sexually ruined for him—but perhaps to this *revista,* that tan woman of thumb proportions depilating herself on page 34?

The phone rang and Mono picked up.

It wasn't Majorie but Methyl.

Which was good news—Mono having had no income in over a week. Had all of Jersey stopped getting—depilated?

I'm coming over, Methyl said.

Under the cashmere overcoat Methyl wore only a wife-beater, the chest hair coming in spirals like @ signs. Below were baggy jeans and between the jeans and beater was a full foot of red boxers exposed.

He came swaggering into the apartment, sat on the bed—there was nowhere to sit but alongside Mono, Methyl waiting as the TV was repositioned, returned to the floor.

This all? he asked.

Mono asked, That mean you're giving me a raise?

Methyl had in his hands a gaming console as gray as a desiccated brain strangulated in black cords attached to two controllers.

It's a new game, he said, still in development. I gave these city guys some tips on how to make it rawer, they gave me a copy of the beta.

He bent to fit plugs into sockets.

Balancing the console on top of the screen.

The TV showed a brick wall.

A man walked past the wall. Another man passed by the wall in a car. The man in the car lowered his window, yelled something indiscernible—*Hooooooo!?!?*—pumped one shotgun round that struck the walking man in the no longer walking head. The car continued, drove offscreen. The man's head broke apart, spattering the wall in seven spots of sanguinary graffiti that dripped down to form a word with seven letters: *Corners*.

Kids crept up to the corpse, pulled spraycans from the pockets of puffies and tearaway trainers and tagged the brick.

One wrote *1 Playa*—effective aerosol sound effect—the other scrawled *2 Playas*.

I play the dealer, Methyl said, you play the snitch.

The screen was splitscreen so there wasn't one wall now but two and they were different.

I'm gonna let you walk free for a while, Methyl said. Try and get a feel for the controls.

Mono the snitch walked to the end of the wall, which was the end of the sidewalk. He walked to the end of the screen but there was more screen. The next block was crowded with bodegary. Fat mamas pushed pushcarts stacked fat with bags of laundry, bags of rice. Hot mamacita hissed. Stolid old guy swept a stoop. Kids, rather trainee cholos, junior bangers.

A red blur burst from behind a tenement's billboard—pigeon graphics flying wildly out of frame as Methyl lunged at his controls, pressed Pause.

This billboard's trying to kill you. Playa's from a rival gang.

Mono asked, What gang am I in?

You used to be in my gang but you snitched me out so I'm trying to kill you too. But also the red niggas want to kill us both. And then the cops. You stay away from cops. I'm taking us off Pause. The second I do just cross the street. Red nigga won't get a clear shot.

Where's the map? Mono asked.

Ain't no map. Just gotta memorize the streets.

Memorize them how?

Lady Liberty knish take the A train, motherfucker! Don't you know New York?

Not the outer boroughs.

We in Manhattan—me uptown, you down. I have it saved in memory to start my every game on 145th and Amsterdam—

Playa 2 starts by default down at Delancey but you can program any block.

Then Methyl quieted and said, Ain't like we in Staten Island.

Snitch heading north up Orchard.

Trendoid gastronomes. Theme outlets that had paid to be included in the game.

Methyl spinning sewer lids like record platters. The soundtrack robotic cucaracha.

Then the snitch stood and did nothing because Mono was watching Methyl's screen half. The dealer was covering major blocks at a major clip shooting everything that moved—everything that moved that was malevolent. He took out pimps in parked cars, slaughtered whole drug deals and arms sales in dumpstered alleys and basements. Wasted lookouts execution-style. Then stole the drugs and arms for later resale. He stopped by a restaurant, ate soul food. He helped himself to seconds, a double order of biscuits to go. He stole a Mercedes coupe and drove off his half of the screen until the two screens converged with the car pulling up on Mono's block.

Mono managed to turn around, fumbled.

Methyl, stepping from the Merc, held his gun sidewise, shot Mono in the face (button A to draw, B to cock to tricksy side, C to pull the trigger).

Screen nasty black with game blood.

You dead, Methyl said.

Me?

You fired too.

I am? I thought you'd come with work.

Methyl sat up, turned to him and said, Any other business you survive this. But the cops today, they online all the time.

People don't know I'm him.

They will.

I'm fucking broke, bro.

The internet says you just that guy who whips it out. But I say you an onus.

Instead of unplugging the gaming console Methyl unplugged the TV, put the controllers atop the console on top, boosted the entire package.

Then he stood on the bed while Mono, getting the silence, got up to get the door.

With the TV's powercord pocketed, Methyl stepped to the floor and walked out to the hall, saying without turning around, I was you I'd start thinking about how to change your name. Bro.

Without the television Mono's apartment seemed both bigger and smaller, and worse.

He should've handled this himself, Mono decided Sunday night when he was down to his last thousand dollars and applying for credit cards online: should've found Em's address or phone through pleading at keggers and honor society socials, then handwritten a letter or called personally, throwing his future on her mercy or just paying her off, throw her a couple hundred or even a thousand—that would've cost the same if not less and less worry.

He shuddered whenever the phone rang.

Majorie? He didn't think Ms. Airline Miles Mogulette ever intended to return his call.

She sputtered, I hope you're not recording this.

I last asked that of you.

Never mind. I've been talking to Tech.

Who?

My support guy.

Who guy?

My computer person.

OK.

But this is mondo illegal, shaky shaky ice. I never said that. I've never done this before.

Done what?

He lit a smoke.

I'm liaisoning with my liaison, my hacker. He's going to hack into this Em woman's blog and erase the original entry then he's going to do the same to all the other sites, I think.

You think? trying to stabilize the ashtray on a knee.

Or else he's going to send them all a virus that destroys everything but leaves no trace, I don't know, I'm no gearhead, just a paraparalegal.

We're talking additional costs?

The tray teetered, heaping.

It's a sliding scale.

A slide beginning where?

We're not prepared to quote just now. We'll send you an email with the figure.

We?

Myself for project management but mostly my tools goon for the tool stuff.

And who is he or she exactly?

Richard, when it's against the law I'm against naming names.

What are the risks?

We assume more risk than do you—that's also why it's expensive, if it's traceable it's to us.

But then you're traceable to me.

Plus it's time intensive—there are worms to code, firewalls to crack.

You sure you know what you're talking about?

It's not a minor undertaking, having to stealthify kludge all that daemon javascript and such—Tech was explaining it all just this morning.

Mono's cigarette was finished except for the filter, the foam pellet he thought of popping into his mouth as if a pacifier, chewy.

I'll call you back when the process is in process, Majorie said. Do you have any payphones in your neighborhood?

I have payphones in my neighborhood.

Find the number of one, making sure it's not the most convenient but pick one a ways far out then email that number to me spaced over ten emails, one digit per email, you with me?

With you.

Then intersperse each digited email with other emails containing links to, I don't care, hardcore penetration, but none of the emails can be sent from your address—be sure to open other accounts with multiple providers.

Didn't I tell you I'm through watching porn?

Then send me more better news, Rich—I have no idea what's happening.

There are wars on.

Mono sent her links.

On Wednesday it felt like winter was finally breaking. The ice could crack for the grass to sprout and a warm breeze could balm the parkinglots and roundabouts and it was fine—winter would be back next year. Mono would be shattered forever.

He put on his coat and walked to the only payphone he was sure of, located just outside the university's main library—every student body could use that phone every day though they never did, they all had phones of their own that didn't require booths. He'd recently forwarded Majorie a link to an article—a web exclusive, never printed in hardcopy—about the phonebook's disappearance. They were going to stop universal distribution—this, the one book everyone could be in.

Students were coming out of the library but none clutched books, they held each other.

And a new beverage for a new generation, not bottles of water but *bottled water,* plastic, perspirant.

They didn't need books because of the bags on their shoulders, which contained computers—tablets and pads on which they could read all that'd been written by anyone ever and also Em on Richard Monomian.

The phone rang but his rush to pick up was unnecessary.

Students, children essentially, pedestrated past as blithe as projected light.

He said, My mailman has no address.

Pigeons alighted on the pathway slabs, pecking at butts and clots of gum.

Was that the password?

You tell me.

We're on track but also delayed.

Which is it?

Both. Plus I need that second thousand.

Behind her speech Mono made out the riddling whir of her computer's cooling fan, the high screech of either passing sirens or neglected pets.

It wasn't that it wasn't spring enough yet or that it was sunset already—he was chilled from being scared, feeling himself recognized by all who passed. He remembered there had been another phone by the gym. Nothing remained besides a stanchion tumescent from a speck of foundation.

Can I call you back from my mobile?

And subvert our subversion—what kind of subterfuge is that?

I'm paying you—so you find a payphone, email me the number, set a time, and I'll also call ten minutes late.

That's precisely what I wanted to talk about. You have my invoice. I have material expenses.

Must be a reason I didn't respond to your email about the next installment.

Richard, it might be better if we talked about this once you're comfortably at home.

Mono had begun to suspect that this hacker of hers, this gensym guru he was never allowed to talk to, was not a person, not a man or woman and so not her lover as Majorie let on, claiming access to him at all hours: when Mono called from home bonged stuporous slack drunk at 3 AM on Thursday asking to be reminded whether they were trying to infiltrate the sites to remove the posts or just crash them with a Trojan she said, Let me ask him. He's sleeping just right next to me. Then there'd be a murmur that had to be her respiration—Mono got the idea she never even took the phone from her mouth to imaginarily rouse this imaginary partner—until she'd say, Tech's grouchy, not getting up. He had a rough day yesterday. I'll ask him over breakfast and check in with you tomorrow.

Mono wondered how delusional Majorie really was, whether she'd invented an illusory male or, worse, she actually regarded her desktop itself as her lover: wedging its switches between her lips and flicking.

On the Friday noon call, which Mono also instigated—Damn, you missed him again! Techie just stepped out for frogurt!—Majorie was saying these blogs had incredible security.

These blogs that were just default regular and free for

anyone to setup and whose platforms required no training for operation and were entirely intuitive to maintain—their protections were just topnotch.

It's amazing, she said, all my attacks are repelled (she'd already slipped into the singular).

Mono grunted.

No offense works, I don't know what's wrong. I've followed all the instructions, took that extra class online, even signed up for the personalized tutorial.

Feels good I'm not the only one being scammed.

Which reminds me, Monday at the latest. Are you sending me my cash?

Monday I'm sending you a sympathy $100.

But there's a program I need.

Your invoice said it was for a line of code.

I need both. Also have to pay the internet bill. Three months overdue. Not everyone's a signal thief.

$100. No more payments after that.

Richard, we're in this together, both our reputations are at stake. She posted my name! my real name!

Her name was Marjorie Feyner.

It was a Wednesday again, a new credit card had arrived, was activated by the ordering of Mexican *muy picante,* and Mono had begun to think about that name change. His computer booted to Word, the .doc scrolled boldly with his mother's maiden name: *White, Richard White, Rich White, R. White.*

In search results for just the word *monomian*—unenriched by Richard—he was still the sixth or seventh, the first five or six being the man who'd named him.

But *Richard White* was limitless—it was a nothing name, a nothing being. There was a Dr. Richard White OB/GYN, a

Richard White, Esq., "Rick" White the builder / general contractor, Richard White the accountant, the actor / voiceover artist, the character in multiplatform franchises, movies, and television shows (the internet tending to catalog other media and not differentiating between an actor's name and a character's), even a Catholic martyr or errant knight—Richard the White?

One self-declared as a pre-op transsexual.

Mono wondered had his father heard about this yet.

This was encouraging, this purity—reboot, restart.

But Mono didn't know what the process was, what documents were needed to make such an alteration official, was about to search for the answer—after anyway replacing his appellation on his most current CV—when the phone rang.

Only one person called anymore, who said, Rich, I have another solution.

Try me.

I've had enough of this cracking crap—this password guess where you're given ten attempts at access then the account's frozen when you fail. Let's get back to the proven methods.

Which methods would those be?

Mono got out of bed, determined he needed more room for his cynicism, opened the door and walked out to the hall. A dull clatter at his sneaks, he swerved to avoid the neighbors' leaky trashbags, greasy bikes.

What's that noise? she asked.

I'm going out for air.

He walked down the hall to the door to the staircase, down the two tottering flights to parking—entirely vacant at midday, it was a lot of lot.

The stairs and landing were also cluttered with bikes—inextricably engaged, their wheels, pedals, gears—locked to the railings. Mono maneuvered, steps following him, steps just behind him.

Suddenly he realized he'd ripped his phone from the wall with the charger still attached. He'd been dragging the cord behind him and turned to pick it up, stashed the scraping prongs and whatever length he could into his jeans' pocket.

Rich, she said, I finally decided to forgo the protocols and searched around for variations on Em—any Emma, Emily, Emilia, or Embeth @ princeton.edu. You're not supposed to do that. Every resource says it's better to abstract the adversary, best to keep them symbols: IP or an email. Person to person, face to face, that's the nuclear option—no other way to go.

I searched that two weeks ago, Marj. You know how many Emmas and Emilys go to Princeton?

I found about 100 possibilities.

99 more than necessary. And before we go any further, tell me this, there was never any tech guy—it was all you just studying up.

Rich, forget Techie. He's over. Moved out. I've moved on. The circumstances have become exponentially more dire. My name's all over the net. Another blog even uploaded a pic of me fatass at the beach. From Richter, Richter, Calunnia, & Di'Famare's summer Law Lounge back when I was still employed.

Mono had to restrain himself from running inside, finding the image himself.

You checked all 100? he asked.

I plugged all their names into the usual social sites, opening a few false accounts to lurk. I took pains, signed in strictly from public connections. One persona joined the Princeton Jell-O polo team, another a networking group committed to combating squirrel chlamydia on campus. Then I got inspired: I opened an account under the real name and title of a real person who didn't have an account—an associate dean of academic affairs who taught undergrad humanities—who'd turn down a friend request from her? She asked to be friends with all the Ems, which gave me access to their profiles.

Impressive, Marj, but what did you find?

She's an Emmanuelle. I've emailed you her profile pic. When you get home I want you to verify then delete.

I'll be home in a second, Mono hurried back upstairs.

If you don't respond I'll know it's her.

You can just stay on the phone with me for another minute and I'll tell you right away.

Mono quickened through the hall.

First he googled images of "Marjorie Feyner," uncovered that shorefront snap. She engulfed a bikini, held a plastic coconut, a fake hairy ball stuck with a straw. People were laughing in the waves—waves of surfboards and tubes—not laughing at her.

Everyone but her was tattooed.

Mono said, Bad strength of connection today. xxxprs laptop-BCrib, what a weakling.

In a new window a pic unfurled, Mono tugging its edge taut.

So? Marj asked.

It's her.

Here Em was, but pixilated younger, with shorter blonder hair hanging in wiry bangs. Braces like microchips programming an exaggerated dentition.

She was deep jawed, Mono recovered the memory—a mouth of gluttonous proportions.

She's a sophomore, major undeclared. I called the school, said I was her grandmother.

You should go easier on yourself.

I told school I wanted to send her a surprise package but lost her address—said I'd found her baby booties, stuffed them silly with favorite candy. The workstudy brat said it wasn't their policy to relay that information. She suggested I call her parents—be in touch with your daughter, with your son-inlaw, she said.

How responsible.

So I searched her friends and identified her high school, searched the local phone listings and called who I thought was her mom.

You what?

Said I was a high school acquaintance of Em's just transferring schools—I positively detested it at Georgetown—and did you have her address as I wanted to get together?

You know—for a drink, take some pills, go to a club, have some seat-down bathroom cunnilingus?

The mother offered her email but I said I'd prefer her street address as my computer had just crashed—it's tragic, I lost everything.

You're jinxing yourself.

She asked wouldn't I rather she give me the phone.

Wouldn't you?

I was afraid it'd be a mobile but she gave me the land-line too.

And you did a reverse lookup?

I had to look up how to do a reverse lookup. You'll find both on my next invoice itemized separately.

And you're going to call or send a postcard? Or go over there yourself?

No.

Don't tell me I should go.

No I've met a new man. I call him Alban. He's Albanian.

He works security at my multiplex for the big crowds on the weekends. I'm always wasting Sundays and we talk. He lets me into a double feature no problem. I made a quiche for him last week.

Not Alban, his real name was Enver. He was a recent immigrant, born in Tirana. He worked for a security company that had classified his language skills as Minimal. Before moving to the area he'd lived in New York, which is where all immigrants live until they sleep with their brother's wife. Enver was not even attracted to her.

His brother's couch was three-cushioned, comfy. And his job, his first job his brother vouched for him, wasn't bad. Enver worked for a friend of his brother's at a pizza joint called, coincidentally, Two Brothers. Albanians being swarthy and proximal to the Mediterranean by birth pretending they knew their dough and cheese and sauce. But Enver wasn't allowed to make the pies. He was supposed to sit on a stool by the back door, held ajar by cinderblock, waiting until his brother's friend's minivan appeared on his monitor. Then he was to open the door all the way, accepting from this man, Arben, whatever he was handed. Electronics, often bags containing something that looked like flour but was not—it was heroin—and less often, bags filled with cash (the entire ring was busted).

Enver was lonely in Brooklyn. His brother came home late from Manhattan. His cousin in Staten Island hated Brooklyn. His cousin in New Jersey hated Staten Island. Enver understood no relevant geography. Across the way was a hair and nail salon. That's it. No other fact or germane sensation.

He tried to make friends. Like when that one time he was allowed to work the register he didn't charge three kids for three slices plus diet grape sodas.

They looked hungry, Boss, he said to his boss, a taciturn elderly American with an erratic scar across his neck in the shape of a dollar sign who was the only employee permitted to make the pies and the next time Enver was in back watching the monitor and the minivan pulled up, when he opened the door Arben smacked him in the mouth and said, You looked hungry.

Arben said that in this language.

One night Enver spun home, spread himself like a fine crust on the couch and started watching—the TV, like the fraternal oven, was always on.

Appropriately disappointing: it was a cookingshow, the woman in it was cooking.

Liridona, wrung from the shower, sat next to him.

The recipe was just some simple stirfry.

Peel your vegetables but lose your nutrients.

By the time the show had cut to commercial Liridona's robe was floored.

Next morning he left for Jersey, pawning himself off on a cousin. His brother never found out, that's why Enver was still alive with intact knees.

Enver said to his brother, Time for you to have babies, as if that explained his abandonment of the couch.

He went to sit for that test at a security company his cousin's friend moonlit for, went to a stripmall themed Early American Grange, sat at a desk exposed to a recently foreclosed storefront's glass—a former florist's still perfumed—and pondered the questions.

They could use him, they explained, as store security—that was the best job, requiring some sort of intelligence and special training—with the worst being crowd control: bars and nightclubs, live events. Almost everyone was retired law enforcement. The proctor, a tubby Hispanic kid who taught communication skills at a community college (a frustrated standup comic), kept calling him "Erven," then "Mile High" because the corrected Enver sounded like *Denver.* They laughed through the exam. "Juan will be back _____ fifteen minutes." (A) in; (B) on; (C) with; (D) about.

Freshly flowering bushes and trees went out of their ways to impress beauty on the youth—the scads of polished khaki kids stalking the kempt paths, groping in the topiary. A frisbee flew overhead. Birds high up enough resembled frisbees. Another class earning credit by punting at soccer. Extraneous jackets were laid out for impromptu picnics. Water bottles wafting clarifying alcohol. A girl smoked a cigarette wedged between her girlfriend's toes.

She came out of Reading Freud PSY 23090, unbound from Green Hall and onto the green, headed toward Chancellor for a coffee. Did she want it iced? Indubitably. Anything to go with that? No that will be all. It was like a phrasebook come to life. What a terrifically executed textbook exchange, why thank you.

Emmanuelle wore mosquitoeye sunglasses, a tshirt whose logo read *Brand,* her skirt never showed lines, no underwear map.

While she waited for change her phone rang, she took the call (from friend R., poli sci major, public health minor, in the midst of a shaming crawl back from a date the night before with a 33 year old iBanker in the city), skimmed milk into her coffee and half a packet of artificial sweetener without bothering to stir.

At the testudinal traffic light she crossed.

College students driving adult cars, vehicles actually too fancy for any adult and perhaps better never driven. They drove them impulsively, alternately absent then reckless as if they already had jobs to get to.

Nassau Street laid the boundary of campus.

Em caffeinated while walking, hollowing her cheeks, pursing for suction then chatty again. Such oversize overactive labials. Let's imagine the waves radiating from her phone—what if they were visible? what if they were colored by her mood? Rainbows, refractive rainbows. Wavelets of talk coursing through the air, coursing daily through our own ears and mouths and minds—yet we're never privy to that talk. Or we'll become privy only when it develops into tumors on the brain.

Retail gave purchase to the quieter suburban.

At a corner with a receptacle she stopped, sipped her last, tossed the coffee inside—not a trashcan but an empty newspaper vending machine.

The day was warming, still not warm enough for flipflops—Em's thongs to soles athwack.

She took two more blocks then rounded the corner: Victorians—two floors, three floors—windows that hadn't been cleaned in failed semesters, porches in a slump. Stoops stooped. The lawns diseased.

Em stopped to tuck phone between ear and shoulder, scratched in her handbag for keys.

Enver crossed the street and waited at the bottom of the stoop until Em turned the key in the lock then he took the stoop in two steps and once on the porch gave her a smile of glittering fillings.

She kept the door open for him with a flipflop. Thinking he was the roofer?

She was still on the phone but on hold. (Her friend's banker date had called, the slut beeped over.)

Enver entered, held the door.

She had a teensy stud in the left naris, a diamond pimple.

He waited for her to check mail.

Yes? Em turned to say, flicking hair into a quote behind the uphoned ear.

Enver closed his eyes.

He couldn't talk while looking at her sunglasses.

What do you want?

She flipped shut her phone.

He said, I want you to change your blogs—opening his eyes only after remembering what Marjorie had told him—I want you to take what you say on your blogs about Mono Man down.

Excuse me?

She dropped the coupons received to the vestibular rug.

And then, he said, to send email saying this was wrong and made up by you to everywhere also.

Also?

Linked, he was straining, posted.

That's impossible! flipping open the maw of her phone, with hardbitten pink polish pressing three buttons then the most commodious, Send—and when she repeated, I want you to know how impossible that is! Enver knew she was stalling, for time, to call, the police.

He swiped at her phone, knocking it to fade its ring through the air as she kicked him with a flipper all gawky, sending her off balance—tricky this kicking in a skirt—and though he put out a hand and caught her before she fell, which must've been his attraction to her, which must've been his, he knew the word from the only other language he knew besides this minimal language and Albanian, *tendresse* (there was so much his brother didn't know that came to light in court: he'd labored a full year in Marseille), with his other hand he made a fist and punched her, driving his knucks into her skull cradled by his hand.

From the floor the ringing continued.

A CCTV camera awning a deli two blocks east caught him on the run—add that to the testimony of Em's neighbor, a spooked Korean grad student Enver thrashed past on the stoop, spilling the kid's bachelor cold groceries: fruit and cereals, sprouts, soy yogurt.

Ludicrous to go back to campus—cameras, everywhere, had him everywhere, running between surveillances. Cutting between frames.

He was as big as a movie to the cops, who had him in custody within three hours (picked up hiding in a basement playpen at his cousin's in Plainsboro).

At the Biergarten I paid for Mono's beers then checked my phone. I'd missed a few calls, had a few messages. Parents, delete. My landlord wanting to make a final Prussian inspection of the premises once my duffels had been shipped then get my keys. Girls, including one Amsterdam video artist with whom I had one unfilmable night. Do not del. The more attractive waitress, the Turk, was attempting Russian with the Russian, saying their *do svidaniya*. A foosball careered across its tabled pitch. A slot machine clanked from the interior dank.

Mono said, Naomi.

She was Mono's cousin on his mother's side.

They hadn't spoken in years—Mono had last seen Naomi at his mother's grave—yet it was she who saved him.

Both sets of parents had emigrated together, had already settled into Jersey and Ph.D. programs by the time they were Mono and Naomi's age, both had graduated together (1982), had bought their houses and had their children at the same time (Mono and Naomi were born the same month, 1984), bought their BBQs, bought their inground pools, opened their email accounts—Mono related the success of this parental relocation, especially successful when compared with ours.

Though Naomi, unlike Mono, was said to have matured.

She was to marry a man so incidental to even his own self let alone to this tale that his name shouldn't be recorded— let's have tact, let's try for it.

About two months before Mono's exploits went viral Naomi's mother called to announce the nuptials and guilt him into being there—New York—the tacky boathouse in Central Park.

She jotted his address for a formal invitation, said, We'll catch up at the ceremony.

Mentioning, There's a girl I'd like to introduce you to. She's a nurse. She looks like A. Jolie.

I'm excited, was all he could say.

She said goodbye with: I called your father for your number. Don't worry, the Poz is not invited.

Poz being Armenian.

Mono, who did not speak Armenian, knew it meant dickhead or equivalent.

Imagine gripping the back fat of that nurselet for the slow dances or having to replay the act behind his meme fame for his smuttier uncles in the bathrooms between the entrée and dessert—Mono didn't want to go, but he had to go: he'd already RSVP'd.

Still he procrastinated, waited until the Friday before the event to ball his only suit into his backpack—the suit black crisp funereal, bought for his college interview—and drive out to find the drycleaner's.

He remembered a cleaner's adjacent to a tanning salon or ye olde historic sandwich shoppe.

Or else adjacent to both.

He didn't google, wished to locate by memory alone.

An hour later returning, having stopped at a diner to park a reuben in his gut.

His suit would be ready only on Sunday, they opened at noon. He'd have to crawl into the suit in the car on the way to the bus or the train.

Out on the patio it'd become a clear summer night—not cloying anymore but breezy perfection—I couldn't believe I had just a week of this left.

The smoke of our cigarettes the only clouds of the moon—closing time.

We were the only customers.

I wanted to offer Mono to pick up his suit, send it to him—airmail? or boat rate?

On me.

We haven't been in touch.

Mono said:

Squadcars surrounded his building. He knew they were idling for him. For dealing, for whatever Marjorie Feyner had done—he didn't know Em was in a coma until resettled abroad, his second night insomniac in Paris when he'd checked that life online at a café.

Circling back, circling the lot.

His backpack was slung over the back of the passenger seat and inside the pack was his passport, which clinched it (the last codex, his last account, those durable blue covers).

They could have his computer, have bed and bare walls.

His password, his password for everything, was *sdrawkcab* (remember it "backwards").

He drove his mother's car to Newark International, abandoned it in Parking. He wasn't in any databases yet. A ticket would be sold.

McDONALD'S

I'd been writing a story, yet another shitblast of the hundreds I've begun only to crumple for ply (I'd never been blocked before, some blockage should've been good for me but), came to that part in the story and just—I just had to stop, it was ridiculous!

I came to the point I knew would come, the point that kept coming, the point where I'd have to say what I didn't want to say, to say what I couldn't—what had no place in, forget my story, I told my father, What I'm talking about has no place in my life!

What are you talking about? Dad asked and smiled retirement's bridgework at being confronted by something as stunningly tedious as himself, probably—but himself fictionalized, as a fictional character—because I'm broke and so was wearing his clothing, also I have the beard he has because we both have weak chins. I'd come back to Jersey for the weekend to sleep without siren in my old ugly unrecognizable bedroom and fill up on homecooking.

I said, I can't say the Word.

We were in the bedroom.

He sat on a chair across from me on the bed and sipped from a wineglass and stared.

I said, You're trying to get me to say it.

The walls were white scuffed with recent paint slashes: color swatches my parents were considering for the bedroom's repainting, assorted pastels and other near neutrals very much not me. The bed and chair were not mine but new. My hutch desk was gone along with the shelving, the room was being converted into a guestroom but—as Mom had strained to say over the phone that early Friday—I would always be welcome.

How can you tell me what happened without telling me what Word? Dad asked suddenly standing older and grayer and rounded goutish and taking his glass from the sill and tipsy but maybe his feet were asleep walked out of the room.

After dinner Mom disappeared sinkward to rinse and call back a friend who'd called interrupting stroganoff, while Dad and I stayed seated as if extra table legs and he said, Let's try this again, so I told him the story:

I said, There's this girl, we'll start with her, I guess I have to describe her. She's pretty? Dad asked, I said, I describe her as *tawny* (I wasn't quite sure what that meant), with red hair dyed and two huge mouthsized eyes. She's sexy? Dad asked and shot a look at Mom who was busy making a dietetic dessert sandwich of ear and phone and shoulder. I said, She's like the girl next door to the girl next door, meaning she's somewhat trashy but also covered entirely with blood, in the first scene she's just bloody head to toe. Of course she is, Dad said (distracting himself with the bottle, he poured the last petit noir), but you can call the different sections of a book, scenes? I thought that term was just for the movies? I said, You can say scene about a book but if you say chapter about a film people will think you're an asshole. Of course they would, Dad said then took a sip winking and by the time he'd replaced empty glass to tabletop the sink had stopped, the kitchen was empty and Mom was already upstairs, her laughter floating distantly and then disappeared, aerated into a higher hilarity—into the refrigerator's hum, the run of the dishwasher, the clock's compulsive perk.

She's in the backseat bouncing, I said, that's the opening: her body bloodied with a knife sticking out of it in the backseat being bounced between her seatback and the backs of the seatbacks in front of her— Wait, Dad asked, what the hell? I said, If he's not careful on the next large preggers bump her corpse could tumble to the floor, falling atop the filthy mats, atop the sloppy wads of mats, to wedge between her seat and his recline.

His? Dad asked, I said, If he doesn't slow down.

It's night? Dad asked, I said, Yes or virtually, the sun's gone down, moon's gone halved, how'd you know? her body's rolling and thumping.

What's the night like? Dad asked, I said, It's wet, the stoplights flash above like spotlights.

It's green, a bright go green, the car's being driven fast.

Slow down, Dad asked, who's driving?

Her boyfriend.

Boyfriend?

Driving southwest, I said, away from the towns he'd grown up in, toward the towns she'd grown up in, poorer to rich, criminal to just criminally tame—quarter tank to Empty, burning last gas, he's wasting time, he's stalling.

Dad asked, What's his name?

Blood's pooling in the seams of the seats, blood's puddling and the radio's off but he turns it down anyway, that's a good detail that he can't stand all that noise, he's turning the volume down, down, lower down, all this one paragraph he's just lowering the volume.

Why's he doing that? Dad asked, I said, It's a circular motion like how you're supposed to stab someone then diddle the wrist, tweaking the knob of the liver, the spleen.

That's a good detail? Dad asked.

Neon sizzles past, neon sizzes, *zisses?* The windshield, in reflection, becomes signage. His throat burns, the boyfriend's, "his hands are readied tense."

It's when I wrote that line—beginning the story from the middle, I realized—that I knew I was stalled too (my hands were *readied, tense*): knew that I couldn't say the Word, knew that I couldn't bring myself to care enough about this Word to write a story with it in it (anyway the Word was not a word, was actually less than a word, was meaningless, had no untainted derivation, had no true legacy or beauty, it was even less than its least letter, it was nothing, it was ruination).

So I described things, I made things up and described them to my Dad: light and signs and the throats of boyfriends, frisking my face in my sleep with a thumbnail that left wounds, smoking quit cigarettes and drinking nightly a half bottle gluglug of whiskey, waking up late so getting to work late where I'd spend Midwestern quantities of time on the internet pursuing this one particular commenter I thought common to a spate of local sports blogs but under twelve different, differently gendered aliases and product recall news especially when it concerned the domestic automotive industry and searching search engines for "whats wrong with my story?" coming back from work still worrying the story and hating the story and thinking that introducing this Word into the story would be like introducing Mom who really wants grandchildren to a girlfriend who's really a man, it'd be like inviting friends over to my apartment for dinner then serving them individual portions of my feces garnished with poems about how much I hate friends and the poetry would rhyme.

It'd be wrong to bring this Word into my story and so into my life, not interesting in the way that foreigners tend to enliven a host country with their cuisine and dress, religiosociocultural traditions and languages, but in fact evil and destructive, The boyfriend's foreign? Dad asked, I'm trying to tell you the story by not telling you the story, I said, you should be aware that this is what writers regularly do, This is America? Dad asked—To recap, I said, he's driving because her corpse is in the backseat and her corpse is in the backseat because he killed her.

The boyfriend might be, I said, he originally was or should've been, I said, heading over to her house, in through the front door then up the stairs to search through her bedroom's drawers for the ring he'd bought her, the ring she'd accepted and that the moment she'd accepted he'd wanted back, not the ring but the money it represented, the overtime it represented, What does he do for a living? Dad asked, But he can't just butt into her house unannounced pushing past her family because she lives with her family now heading upstairs to go through her bedroom's drawer, I said, construction, he works construction, What kind of construction? Dad asked, He killed her with his switchblade, I said, which he keeps in a jacket pocket.

He stabs her with a switch just to get a ring back? Dad asked, But that's where the quandary squats, I said: He's been driving around for an hour, driving around for hours with the corpse in the back thinking to himself what to do what to say, should he ditch the body and where or bring it with him indoors while early evening remains, smashing into her house at what could conceivably still be dinnertime with the nice dishes out, the whole bird starched for the carving, the veggie sides to the side, no flowers but flower motif vase (narcissus), (snuffed zircon-encrusted) candlesticks without candles—to innocent and gentle with grace lay her body like a fine polish atop the diningroom table, to force her father to cover her body with a tablecloth "as if a bridal gown," the detail, the cloth "lawned in dewsmoothed white," the poetic description, or else he could, he thinks again another alternative, leave the body in the car, go inside the house alone and without explaining anything not to the victims neither to the reader slaughter everyone inside because her family—father, mother, four grandparents like a full set of heirloom silver—would be the only people who'd miss her if she went missing, What's her name? Dad asked, what's his? I said, And to die is to go missing profoundly, When and where's this set? Dad asked, what kind of car's he driving? Or maybe it'd be better to narrate this chronologically, I said, Dad asked, Chronology means you're finally going to tell me what happened?

Ray, I want to call him, or Ronald, I said—though other options are Mac, Dick, Donnie/Donny, Smith/Smyth(e), Luke, and John—but she I'm convinced is a Patty because there's something in her face like an underdone hamburger patty, like its waxed plastic wrapping, or a mess of wet napkins smeared with makeup sampled from a mortuary for clowns, I thought you said she looked good? Dad asked, She has a hot body, I said, a hot little body, a hot tight little body but the clownface is unfortunate, kind of greasily melting and the car is a Ford, What model Ford? Dad asked, A white Ford, I said, a white Ford Escort, I said, I don't know why I have such an easy time saying Ford but I do, it's simple to say and so obvious to say the car was a Ford and it was, maybe a Ford Fiesta in red, in yellow, in a color like Autumn if Autumn's a color—do Fords come in Autumn? is it redundant to speak of an Autumnal Ford? Dad (who might, as I write this, be performing his nightly check that the garage door is locked) asked, Why would you have trouble saying Ford?

Mac, Dick, Mick, Ray Ronald, or let's stay with Ronald Ray, I said, who's driving this—no forget I said Ford, it just sounded reliable, authentic or verisimilar, a moment ago but now it sounds shitty.

I'm not following you, Dad asked, what's so shitty about Ford?

Me, I said, past tense:

Ronald Ray left the house he and Patty shared, the house they used to share until last week's fight over when and where to hold the wedding—Patty was always fighting for later and splurgier—caused him to hurl a boot at her: him awhirl in a single sock, kicking her out of the house—with an eye that would bruise orifically black, a parturient bust lip—her calling her parents from a payphone two corners down to come collect her but not letting them call the police. The house was a rancher, the rancher didn't have a driveway, Ronald Ray kept the car out front, he walked to the car, there was a busstop out front and the car kept getting nicked by the bus, the bank owned the car, the bank owned the house, he leased both from the bank, the bank owned the block, This isn't the city? Dad asked, He didn't have any work that day, I said, he had the day off because there weren't any construction jobs because no one was building anything because no one had any money and the banks weren't giving loans, Even though the tense you're using is past, Dad asked, are we still talking about the present? He got into the car and drove into town from their suburb, I said, and while nondescript is itself a description that's how it'll be described initially, just by the way it's written it should be obvious that there is no town, that this town is rather all suburb, that there's no middle, no coagulant center and that the more Ronald Ray drove he never got any farther from the house just more involved in the grid, more involuted and lost and it seemed like hours though it was only minutes, it seemed like an entire afternoon though it was at most half an hour until he pulled up in front of a diner, A diner? Dad asked, Ronald Ray idled there, I said, watching through the plateglass printed with greedy full palms of fondle his girlfriend or fiancée or, screw it, wife enough Patty finishing her shift and just when the news blared he turned the radio off, looked up from the dial and there was the climax of the story.

The climax? Dad asked, I said, It all has to be in the mood or tone if there's anything distinguishing mood from tone or in the way that waitressing Patty leaned like a wiperag hanging from the window's backpocket—leaned across the counter to swipe herself out for the day and her manager, that's how he's characterized, "her manager," rushed over and pinched her but she straightened out and smacked his hand from pinching again and went to walk out the door to stand at the busstop and this, this harassment, was daily, Whose harassment? Dad asked, did her murderer pick her up usually? He pulled around the block to pull up alongside her at the leafpiled curb and that shocked her, I said, she didn't know what to do or say but acted like he hadn't just witnessed what happened, maybe he'd missed it or would forget that he hadn't with the sunglasses over twelve stitches smile she gave as she opened the door and got in, but as soon as she was seated and had shut the door she knew that he'd seen it because he leaned over the stickshift to kiss her, which is something he never did, that not being the kind of thing this character would do, Why not? Dad asked, what's he scared of? But this kiss—"this pinch of lips" "this stitch of kiss"—was only a diversion, I said, because with one hand on the wheel he stabbed her, stabbed her with his switch and she screeched and overtop the casualty of her screech the tires smoked as he shifted to streak away, straightened the car and pulled his knife out of her then her body toward him to toss over the median stick into the backseat where she rolled and thumped, the knife he dropped to the floor unwashed white, washed in red with the knife kept inside her body thumping and rolling around the backseat slicing the wound open wider to pour its packet of ketchup—"that condiment the color of love," And he did this why? Dad asked, I can't understand his motivation, I said, If I wanted to

have a body thumping in the backseat of a car, the car had to
be in motion and the body had to be dead, and if I wanted
the body to be dead, Patty had to be killed, So you began
this whole thing just to have a body bumping around? Dad
asked, Like the secondhand of a clock, I said, the sweeper-
hand if you want to get poetic about it, like the Atlantic
lapping against a jetty or your testicles slapping up against
a woman's own backseat as you rut at her sexually from
behind, Do you always just write from or toward one idea?
Dad asked, and is that one idea always so fucking moronic?
But the idea was for the body's bump to symbolize time,
I said, and while the sound is time ticking the image isn't
so much the dead body as it is the car driving around with
the dead body inside, rolling and thumping and thumping
and rolling, So you have all that to what end? Dad asked, I
said, That's probably when the monologue comes in, when
Ronald Ray whose name makes him sound like a multiple
killer already and who certainly looks like a killer with his
bleared face but whetsharp nose tries to figure out what to
do in first person, not just what to do with the body like
should I chop it up somewhere abandoned and into what
amounts but also what to do in the aftermath, how to feel,
crank the tears, check under the hood for a heart or soul,
consternation Ronald Ray—this is the junction in the story
where I/he make(s) plans and alibis, complots turned con-
spiracies for the authorities and surviving fam, Like what?
Dad asked, Like I was going to pick her up at the diner and
she saw me and was running to me across the street waving
when she was hit by a car, a van or truck that said across the
side of its haul Someone's Grocery, like I just showed up to
pick her up and was waiting for her running to me waving
when a man came around the corner he was Afric I think
to sink like this knife into her incalculable times until she

expired there in my arms dragging her into my car, which is why I didn't call an ambulance, But does she have to die? Dad asked, does she have to die so terribly? But death on the page is just a typo, I said: You can't say for example, *She is dead*—"she" no longer *is*. You can't say for example, *She was dead*—death itself, a condition coterminous with eternity, renders the past tense inaccurate. But what does it mean that death is just some sort of mistake? Dad asked, some only known to writers language error? But there is no Dad, there never was any Dad, my own father would never ask such questions, my own father would never have had the patience to listen to me talk about literature let alone about my own literature or murder and sex in some ineptly imagined Midwestern state though I think that unlike the after-dinner drunk sextalk about rear entry testicular thwacking, which would've offended him, the violence would've only made him uncomfortable (Are you sure his car's a manual transmission? is something he might ask, however, Why not just make it an automatic and not have to deal with the shifting, the shifts?), just as certain other things unsettle me, certain things and times and places, the here and now and *certain Words*.

Ronald Ray drives, Mom. Lights sparkle as they shoot across his glass. A compact car filled to spill with hemoglobinic wine. When do lights become light? Can something that sparkles also shoot? Mom, you used to be able to answer every question lightly. Ronald Ray passes trees. He passes a mailbox flagged with wilting balloons. Why do balloons wilt (I was six when I asked that)? How does the mail know how to get from Popop's house to us (I was four when you took me out to meet the mailman)? He passes a theater marquee advertising the year of my birth, also the year of his and Patty's for convenience. What is parkinglot and what not? Which is tree and which just pole for phones?

Mom, he drives and I leave him driving to call you Hello, calling you not on your workphone because it's too early for work but on the homephone because Fridays you don't work but are up early out of habit and I listen to you talk, to your stories about your old friends I don't like—who have children my age whose successes I don't like—about your new friends whose names I don't recognize, to what you're cooking as if smell travels through newer model phones, I listen to recipes and your dairyfree, glutenfree modifications, about the trip you're planning to the Santa Fe Aunts, the intermediate pottery class you're taking and the inflammatory bowel disease support group you volunteer with and he drives. He is as lost as a 1:1 map—whereas I'm still only partly awake, despite this being a call I initiated, a call I now want to end, I have to be at work in an hour (and I'm fresh out of gunpowder—the tea).

This is like the Ford, Mom, as it involves other names. It involves what I've told you and what I haven't and just like mothers lie to children not only about where air goes to and mail and phonecalls come from but also about difficult subjects like death and God and can God die? most children lie to parents too, though my lies have been mostly moronic—mine have been lies of omission (and so you can understand why I've forgotten to tell you about them until now). I've told you I work at a pharmaceutical company, a few times I might even have said *a pharmaceutical multinational*—as if the sum of the countries malignly conspiring factor into my salary—but what I haven't told you is that I work as a proofreader. That's it, as a copyeditor, the lowliest of editors, a reader not even a writer, I'm not allowed to write, I've never met the writers. Their copy just shows up in my 9 AM email from close of business in Delhi or Lahore, and I'm supposed to go through it—the label materials, the innards instructions for use—and mark mistakes. It doesn't take a native to spot misspelled symptoms and dropped articles *the* and *an,* but it does take a native to sweat being outsourced every quarter (will Lahore proof Delhi? or Delhi proof Lahore?).

When I began my story I was proofing a drug called Nomenex, Mom—it's supposed to make you "happier" (my word), maybe it does, probably doesn't, but efficacy isn't what irks me as Ronald Ray drives. What irks me is how people in the office still talk about it. If an officeperson is in a bad mood, Mom—say they've misfed their pets or their siblings have been imprisoned, leading them crying to handicapped toiletstalls and service stairwells to be used only in case of cardiac exercise or emergency, for private phonecalls to haute veterinarians and obscure lawyer uncles—they don't say, She might need Nomenex, or, You might want to ask your doctor about Nomenex, they say instead, She needs to get Nomenexed, they say, Nomenex her, or, Nomenex the bitch, and people will even say that about themselves, Nomenex me, I'm a week behind, I assfucked my diet, can't sleep, and Heather hates me. Heather or weather or whatever depresses, Nomenex my ex while you're at it. My coworkers all have names like Heather, Mom. How can you be a person with a name like that? how could you expect to be an original individual? Names aggregate, exaggerate, caricature everything too explicit. Two Ricks in Accounting. We all know Ricks, even Rick knows what to expect from a Rick. Marketing Steve. It's fairly obvious how to market a Steve. Tucson, indisputably itself (handles distribution), Trenton sweet Trenton, the transparent worst ("our" lab), Ronald Ray drives and Patty patters.

Mom, I dress in whatever's clean. Pants, shirt to which the tie's always tied and buttoned into collar, jacket single-breasted, all of it solidcolored except the tie hoisting miniature flaglike stripes, red fimbriated white, the pants dark to where I can't tell blue or black, the shirt white disclosing dull stars of dribbled deli coffee, jacket matching pants whether exactly or inexactly depending on blue or black, socks definitely black, shoes definitely black (these last were bought together and the salesman gave his word)—what definitively coordinates this colorwise already possibly coordinated wardrobe is that all its brands are utterly defunct. Dad having brought them over the years to my apartment, Dad having bought them years ago, decades and waistline inches ago, these clothes—now covering the nudity of my apartment that's only a closeted bedroom with bathroom reeking of clogged piping adjoining—mean zero to me, their designers mean zero to me, their normally significant tags giving no contemporary indication as to whether the signified article was once expensively fashionable or just cheap and extraordinarily lame. My other shirts have pips and flecks but no logos, Mom. My other pants are jeans—manufactured in sweatshops sequestered in purdah halfway across the innominate earth—and they certainly have their endorsements, but I purposefully purchase them hidden, to be hermeticized by my belt or within the inseam of the jean, facing the migraine strain of my erection—bet you're glad to have that thought, Mom, as Patty jerks and shudders.

I take the train moving faster than any car traffic moves, without stoplight, without stopsign, but still Ronald Ray is routed reckless and the body humps around. Mom, they remain lost, as do I. Working at a multinational means that I work in only one nation and cannot travel, I commute.

There is a spire often passed. There is an office in the spire oft passed. Not only does this pharmaceutical multinational have a name but its subsidiaries also have names and some of these subsidiaries sell pharmaceutical products with names and other of these subsidiaries license for sale generic versions of pharmaceutical products and even these generics have names (generic names)—and the spire has a name too, and the name of the spire is the same as the multinational's name but before the spire was named for the multinational it was named for a company that was acquired by the multinational and the company's name was added to the multinational's name and so the spire's name, Mom, was accordingly changed, respired (names I cannot mention, names I wouldn't even breathe).

9 AM, booting my workcomputer, my morningcomputer, to remind me of where I'd stopped the night before (I'd never stopped): I didn't know where to bring Patty's body, Ronald Ray didn't know what to say about the body, we didn't know what our responsibility to it was, Mom, with even our tenses undecided. He ranged about their nativity. It was unbelievable that someone could call this fictional strip familiar, but it was also believable. Impossible and yet possible that someone could call this commerce home (I was thinking about home when I wrote that). All around him was Vacancy with the vowels themselves vacant, *Vcncy:* the local errata of burned connections, burnt bulbs, *Free Cable TV!* as if in advocacy—what was cable locked up for this time? (That's a line I'd been saving.) Didn't we already pass this pass, Mom? make that exit or eat a meal? Did we take our meds or no? and if so, shouldn't they have been taken with a meal? Light blinking lights. Mom, does a light blink on or off? or does just saying *It blinks* cover both? This was what I thought about for a week. Blinkblinking go the cor-

rex, the corrigenda. 9:30 email, 10:00 new product slogan session (even us galley drones are polled), 11:00 email, hunger, boredom (which is another kind of hunger), still Ronald Ray was driven and Patty not ceasing to be deceased.

Wednesday without breakfast, I realized he might be hungry too. Thursday with my 11:30 canceled (a standards review, the proctor had the flu), I'd had enough of being desked. I thought, find a place to eat. I thought, find a place to eat, you'll find a place to gorge your story. Not a job to shirk, Mom. Existence was at stake, survival. My own. That of, in motoric italics, *my story*. Murder, a hunger itself, gives such a hunger also. Both being matters of appetite, of denying yourself until you break. Of holding steady the wheel until the engineblock just cracks. Of going further—*farther*, Mom, or *further?* or are they interchangeable like signs, changing only their destinations over statelines? I refreshed my memory of the distinction before heading out to lunch. This was the last day of the first week I was blocked. I went *farther* than I regularly went, Mom, not to belabor this any *further*. I went blocks. I passed restaurantfood, passed barfood, he passed arcades serving arcadefood, passed billiardhalls and bowlingalleys offering billiard and bowling fare. But foodfood, Mom. You could've cooked for him, I could have if I cooked.

Food, the bottomless metaphor. Food like, or as, an insatiable simile. A pocket of inmeats carved from a cart. That was my objective. Courtesy of a sanguine sincere Halali who liked to practice Spanish. The money from every pocket sold went to feed and clothe his wife and son deserted in Halalabad. He'd asked me, What are the foremost headphones to obtain for my heir? what is the most stable skateboard one may acquire? My answer had been to avoid him for a month. Regrets, Mom. I missed his rotisserie physique, the carbonating banter. Standing talking terrorist economies on the corner of 10th Avenue & Inanity—my cart wasn't there, my Spanish Halali wasn't there. I bummed a cig (secretary), a light (deliverer), stubbed. That invaginated pita pocket topped with pickled veg—I'd enjoyed it there before, I would always have enjoyed it there before. Back in the lobby without a meal but within the hour, I surveyed what foodstuffs my fellow spireists preferred. Security pumped dumbbell wraps and protein shakes. 12's receptionist left the elevator at 12 receptive to water and a salad. None of that would do, Mom. Back in my cubicle—Ronald Ray at his windshield, my screen—it took another hour to understand how badly I'd been poisoned.

Mom, I spent the next month stuffed, plugged, in the grip of a pathetic mogigraphia (I plucked a reference text from leveling the fridge in the office kitchenette to determine the technicalese for "writer's block")—unsure, or perhaps all too sure, as to where, precisely, my character should dine. Agonizing over why he would dine there, over what dining there would say about him/me—over which would be riskier: drivingthru a drivethru with Patty in the back? or just parking her carcass for a three course duration? Should he gratify the impulse to return to Patty's diner? or could that be read as too safely laning tragedy between reassuring shoulders? Ronald Ray watched the backlit logos approach, every craven incarnation, every franchise of desire. So many amenities yet so many the same, so many ways to condemn them, yet all of them the same. Too many few choices: which restaurant *I should go to?* what to order at which restaurant *he should go to?* which suit to wear or wash? having skipped breakfast should I skip lunch too to write? I know nothing impresses you, Mom. During lunchbreaks I kept seated, kept him moving. *Me* suffering sedentary in a chair too crippled to swivel, *him* swerving for sushi prepared by Chinese, dialing ahead for Mexicali—but how would Ronald Ray dial, Mom? did he have a cell or would another payphone have to be implicated? I refilled the car with gas, kept his own tank unfulfilled.

By workday's wane when I was supposed to be reproving an unapproved attention deficit aid—"NAME [the Indipaks aren't allowed to know the names of the medications whose materials they assemble by template: names are privileged, to be inserted only by us employees with miles of clearance] may cause side effects. Tell doctor if any symptoms is severe or does not go away: nervousness, restlessness, difficult falling or staying asleep, uncontrollable shaking of a part of the body, change in sex drive ability"—I was having difficulty, Mom, paying attention myself (which is "the cognitive process of selectively concentrating," according to a collaborative website I edited when I should've been otherwise editing, anything but changing that entry to read: "the cognitive process of selectively concentrating on what happened to that shawarma stand on 10th?"). Misprints slipped by, slopping my copy. I was warned, I who typically issued the warnings (that's all my copy was): do this, don't do that, if you experience nausea or upset stomach, with Ronald Ray *dromomaniacal*. The dictionary definition for *dromomania* linked to a thesaurus, which suggested (advised/broached/ commended) *drapetomania* (that quack syndrome that caused slaves to flee captivity). I searched that up, left a page on my screen when I wandered to pee, was reprimanded for my (the subtext was racist) violation of corporate IUP (Internet Usage Policy). At least mine wasn't "painful or frequent urination," though with all this stress—though *affect* is not *effect*—I was experiencing "unusual weakness," which once arrived in an Indipak email phrased as "unusual weakedness"—I'd never be capable, no computer would be capable, of writing as beautiful as that, Mom. I'll never get a raise, or a promotion, and we use what's called the serial comma. I typed pages I trashed, then feeling anxious a co-spirist might find them retrieved them for shredding into piñata entrails, which I bagged in a bag inside a bag to dump to the dumpster of a nonneighboring impasse (if I could've, I would've shredded the impasse).

And this was *every day,* Mom, which is two words when talking about a repeated experience but one word, *everyday,* when speaking of the boring, the mundane. Anything on my workcomputer I'd email from: to: my personal email, delete. Once home I'd check email on my homecomputer, my nightcomputer, reread the day's writing, rewrite. I'd skimp on dinner, email myself the night's skinning and gutting then, tucked between bedsheets lined like obsolesced paper, turn off the light. *Every day* lived double, *everyday* duplicity. Nomenex us both, Mom, but read the smallprint first: Nomenex doesn't exist, it's an exemplar drug, a composite of composites—inspired by how an amphetamine can be combined with a dextroamphetamine into a single drug that both focuses your attention and helps you lose weight, which gives the attention of others something better to look at, someone slimmer on which to focus their own personal doses—a fictional surrogate for an array of antidepressants that actually do exist and that I would prefer not to mention for fear not only of legal reprisal (in case this is published), but also of being fired. I couldn't sleep, Mom, but I didn't need a sleeping aid—I needed a hamburger. I won't be disingenuous, I needed a specific burger—buns and pattymeat indistinguishable, but the burger distinguished by other criteria. I could taste it, Ronald Ray could taste it—could taste its very ingredients active and inactive—but I could not prescribe him what he wanted, what I wanted even: I couldn't Nomenex any of us with nonexistent Nomenex, I couldn't name and by naming bring into being, Mom, I was a wreck.

Ronald Ray, he will try this in third person. There's nothing more efficient than third person (omniscience), and a story about fastfood should be nothing but efficient. The writer—J, say, the fictionalizing illeist, regular masturbator, and underemployee—can write but he cannot name, even though he knows what he wants to name, he knows what he wants to say, he knows the Word, he knows the letters that form the Word, he knows the sounds of the letters and the shapes of the letters, Ronald Ray, he knows them like he knows the word *uxoricide,* like he knows the hard and soft sounds and the shape of the *J,* but he cannot pronounce them or form them in order, he cannot assemblyline them into the . . . he can only have you cruise incommoded, making your mileage, your exits and turns, incarnating yourself and the grid, substantiating yourself within the grid as he maps his own failings—at night with his head centered on the white perfection of pillow that needs only a few scattered seeds and a moment's toasting to resemble a bun—as wars and diseases roil around, bubbling up here and there like effervescing oil. He cannot do it, Ronald Ray, he's sorry but even wretches must have standards, wretched fictional standards. He could invent a fictional restaurant for you to bite your burger at but any fictional restaurant would be, like Nomenex, a worthless simulant or inconcinne imitation, a placebic generic. Any burger restaurant he invents would obviously be based on a real burger restaurant, a real burger restaurant everyone knows and has been to and that even he's been to (the writer has also taken the succedaneous drugs on which Nomenex is based). Pity the burger outlet that must go up against a fiction? No, pity the fiction that must go up against a burger outlet! Ronald Ray, is the writer afraid to be seen as being in the pocket of his fake franchise's competition? but can a chain that doesn't exist have any competition? To invent one restaurant is to flatulate an entire chain? Yes, Ronald Ray, ridiculous! The writer would have to sit in his apartment unpublished (and lately the water pressure's been stingy), and create a burger franchise, create a name and even a logo for it and falsely register and trademark and copyright the entire invention from its appearances exterior and interior to its gastronyms, the hammy neonames of its supersynthesized cuisine and why? only because he doesn't want to be seen as endorsing any actually existing and beloved burger franchise in this crap creatic tale, apologies Ronald Ray, of your girlfriend's hackneyed murder? Does the writer really think that if he mentions that existing famous burger franchise in his story he might help mayospread its fame—spread it like war and disease? like literary "influences"? Is he convinced he'd only further popularize its (he can't decide on the one encompassing word) *homogenization?* is he convinced he'd only further homogenize the utter diversity of its damage? He shouldn't be, he shouldn't worry. This story will never be published, it will never survive—unlike plasticbags, unlike styrofoam, which will degrade forever. This story is closer to what's packaged inside: unhealthy, produced by exploited labor (self-exploited), to be consumed or unconsumed, either way quickly gone, quickly forgotten. Excreted, excreated. Ronald Ray, you must be ravenous. Roll down a window and ponder the polysemy of "draft."

RR, this is what your writer did: He stopped writing and began reading, library books and pages printed from the internet, pages on the internet, all about the history of this burger franchise he was thinking of, this burger franchise that cannot be named (but unfortunately cannot not be thought of) (while the job was ignored, while he neglected his word counts, his presence in the office that of a fussy, persnickety, ultimately rejectable caret, him stetting all carelessness by being careless himself)—reading about the brothers who'd founded a restaurant that made burgers and that was very successful, everyone loved their burgers and came to eat them from all over the area where their restaurant was located, this was California and the year was 1954 (information like a conglomerate restructuring imagination: 1954 the birth of color TV, your writer's parents, desegregation!), and then another man approached these brothers, an entrepreneur with the entrepreneurial spirit, and bought from them their restaurant and along with buying their restaurant did something absolutely incredible—your writer remembers how shocked and incredulous he was when he learned this was possible, he remembers how naive and immature he felt when he learned that not only could this be done but that it was done often and that there were even laws in place to govern such indelible transactions—along with selling this man their restaurant these brothers *sold this man their name.* The burger restaurant's founding fraternity sold their surname to this man who promptly trademarked it, in doing so preventing the brothers from collecting any further monies based on its usage: if they wanted to open another restaurant— emburgered, unemburgered, regardless—they couldn't use their own name, they had to use another, it was almost an indulgence that they were allowed to keep their surname at all, permitted to pass the name of their father as a birthright to their children (did they have any children? check?). This man as sole owner of the patriprefixed name of other men then took this sole restaurant he owned and duplicated it, triplicated it, corporatized the restaurant into restaurants throughout California to begin with before proceeding to culinarily colonize the country and then the world and your writer read about this, RR—this was his only attempt at research and his findings disgusted and that was winter, New York City, 2008.

A winter in which your writer avoided his parents and slacked on his quotas and for environmentally unsustainable months kept you driving insomniac throughout the Midwest or middling enough environs only because he couldn't bring himself to write or type out the novenary letters that nominalized the restaurant you and he so desperately had to patronize, RR—with that body in the back, that bloody body in the back, with the corpse in your trunk, your writer thought, the corpse in pieces pocketed about your person, your writer rethought. The difference between freeway and highway being. The difference between a street and a road is. Verbs: *to vor* at vittles, *to phage* the grub. Adjectives: *wet* highway, *green* highway, *bluegreen* highway, *knotted / involutedly tortuous*. Tolls? (*Incorporate:* the relationship between procrastination and hunger, *image:* radio's volume knob as areola, *image:* roadside ditch like a rumbling fryer, *image:* RR's stomach a spare tire, *image:* in the backseat, only soured leftovers clunking around.)

12/08, pages / .txt files were surfeited with substitute titles for this unnameable pit: *Melter's, Grilltastic, Big Burger* ("Where the Burgers are Big," whose stale logo was to have been two linked *B*s, two interlinked *B*s—like the monogram on a newlywed couple's luxe towel set—until he stumbled on the potential inherent in two *B*s whose long vertical spines had been laid horizontally, lazy recumbent *BB*s suggesting two brothers with beerguts knocked flat on their backs breathing hard after a meal—as if a napkin had been pulled out from under them—or like four stomachswelling burgers queued up for an aftermeal snack: ⌨⌨). The hope was to make art, RR, not problems. Not recipes for prose, not prosaic receipts. Your writer couldn't bring himself to wordprocess the name of this famous imitatee, searching instead for other names to call it, why? he asks himself, Why? Maybe he can't mention the famous out of resentment? maybe he resents everything famous? After all this famous original—he should start calling it differently every time so that not even a reference or negation becomes its appellation by default: Famey Chain, or Fra-Fra-Franchise, Sobriquette, or The Restaurant That Resists All Monikering—after all, this infamous chain has never paid him, this cloying corny syrupy franchise that won't or can't etc. etc. has never supported his art.

RR, your writer is (hopes to be) a writer who writes, not a corner office capitalist on an expense account binge, bibbing himself with stock certificates. Why should he sponsor or be sponsored by that fastfood company by putting its brandname in his story? in yours? Would that foodstuff corporation ever print his scriving on its wrappers? would they festoon their fries containers with the opening of *The Bloody Body?* Could you swallow this, RR? "His girlfriend of the tawny mouthsized eyes," descried across the apple pies, among the chicky nuggets—what tawny fries like fingers! and what a terrible title, *The Body Dies Bleeding!* Maybe your writer's afraid of the present? of the genre of the present (ephemeraphobia)? maybe he doesn't want to date his story? stories should be timeless—anachronistic? The dilemma being that even the slightest details—such as a car and feast of equal speed, pharmaceuticals and spires—serve to date and place a text, fix it in history and geography. Your story's now become *a text,* RR, which is when you know the story's over (it should've been over with that sizzly neon you had passed, neon scribbles everything pluperfect).

RR, maybe your writer's the only writer who has this problem, maybe he's too serious. Possibly other writers have been better adjusted to their circumstances, as people less inhibited. He would ask them if he knew them, knew any intimately enough. Only A.J. of the cursive mustache and Russian obsession (they were in school together, A.J. writes whodunit juvenilia). B.C.D. (another schoolmate hack, she wouldn't dryhump) who profiles for a weekly more read for its less logorrheic cartoons. H. who wrote her dissertation on Nabokov in the voice of Nabokov: fractious, lilting, Germanophonic, Francophonic, superiorly unsuburban, the prize for which is tenure. Y. who doesn't know if the plot he's "fleshing," the flesh he's "developing"—his fiancée has learned to cook from the appropriate TV—wants to be a novel or screenplay. Fear not libel or defamation (I've even falsified initials), literature has lost that power. Fair use means only that the user's unfairly used. Your writer knows visual artists who've sold their bodies to corporations, tattooing emblem and catchphrase on cadaverous forearms and calves. He knows more abstract composers whose music features dissonances that must be endured if only to more fully appreciate the relief afforded by a DJ snippet of pop from the 1990s or '80s or '70s or '60s or '50s. Art that samples other art, quotes that quote other quotes—your writer knows this phenomenon, in jargon *he's aware,* he was raised in a culture of (not more ironic jargon, select only the most appropriate gustatory analogy): regurgitation, a culture of glutting to vomit and glutting again on the vomit until reemesis—chunky cheese mimesis—then licking that puddle again. RR, your writer knows that concepts regarding the usage of brandnames and sundry commercial verbiage in fiction have been thoroughly described by other writers using other words, using long words, multisyllabicized compoundlongfrankfurteresquewords that sound and look on the page as repellent as the copyrighted proper nouns they critique (he won't "instantiate" them here) and, RR, your writer also knows—as fact! as fact! that all his concerns about brandnames & co. are considered old and trite and that most people meaning most of his peers consider him if intellectual then pretentiously stilted (what Y. said when he sent your story to him, "preciously stilted"), grinding and dull (Y. saying, "your story's all grind grind grind and only then, dull"), they think his problem—that writing the name of a profiting entity in a nonprofit or negligibly profitable story causes him pain—is more like an antiproblem, a solution of years ago, a solution of decades ago, that in the very annus Reaganis your writer was born it was already OK to use copyrighted brands in one's art. But what your writer senses now is that it has become not OK anymore and that what once was liberating is now just sad, is now also in some sense controlling. What once transgressed today merely oppresses. (Add a clause to the effect that people don't smoke or drink as much anymore after a century of manipulation by the alcohol/tobacco industries/lobbies) but still writers insist on branding brandnames onto their stories, RR, doing unpaid product placement like this not because to avoid doing so would be incongruous or distracting but because the question to place or not to place does not even occur to them as a question, they'll insert a brand into a story because brands have been inserted into their lives as if through stabbing gavage or rape and have become, what is the banality, second nature, yes, brands have become a second nature to nature and breathing them in as natural as breathing. Today entire sentences can be made by brands jammed like cars, entire paragraphs like crashed cars your writer's rubbernecked—his sore sloucher's neck—on his commute: Redesigned mascot icecreamed telecom spokesperson in re: specialty flavor glitch w/ online airline ticketing. Revise, verise. Make even this technique proprietary. "He would die before he fell in love" translating to, Male celeb *would* [suffer the same fate as (he did in) his previous film] *before he* diamonds / dozen roses / boner supplement champagne. *He checked his* watchbrand. *His smile as sticky as* brand of tape or glue. Your writer is alone, RR, having no wife to carnificate into hamburger meat or future. He has no girlfriend to mold by pattycake into the burger of the future. An aborted novel he has, set aboard a space capsule that was to be revealed at novel's end to have never been launched from Camden. A novella, a novelette, narrating at a page per minute an hourlong pornclip starring a pornstar named Jami Joyce. And this, the story of his neuroses, paranoia becoming a style: He never writes the word *America,* opting instead for allusion or ellipsis; he writes "the City," CAP optional (instead of New York City); he writes "anonymous strip" (instead of I-95, though a foolish instinct counsels: "I-nonymous"); and, of course, he never uses semicolons. And while we're at it, RR, let's insist on "styrofoam," which was likewise left above in lowercase, in minuscule, though it properly should be "Styrofoam™," in majuscule, the term for "extruded polystyrene foam," trademarked by the Dow Chemical Company. Possibly your writer has no reason. Is impractical. Is not practical. Like why, after all this time, is he still writing—"has no reason"—in third person?

I was tired of this, tired of inventing other worlds— "realms," "dimensions," I was *exhausted* by synonym, by quotationmarks too—tired of inventing alternate worlds while misunderstanding my own, yes, yes, but also *I was starving*.

I got up, left the house (apt.).

No more ambiguities. Imprecision renders nothing worthier, nothing universal.

The following writers have worked as advertising creatives: *(fill this in later)*

Nothing universal but, galaxies. Nothing universal but, the universe.

I walked—I mclive in Brooklyn, I mchave no car—to McDonald's. There, there, walked, walked, a welfare visne, nobody has cars, there are barely buses. Gravesend's what it's called, the end of graves, the grave of graves (the British buried atop the Dutch). Cameras surrounded by barbedwire like they were gun installations, protecting. The parkinglot, empty, speckled with gums. Lines for the cars that were missing were black like grillmarks. The drivethru window everyone walkedthru was blacked too. When the shade was down you had to knock. I considered walkingthru myself and knocking, reconsidered. I had to force myself to full experience. "Full-Service"—a euphemism used only by callgirls and restaurants. This was not research but living, this was not living but life.

The location—the door sealing shut, leaving me a victim to airconditioning whose level was set, I believe, by corporate HQ—the physical plant. It smelled like grease, fat / soap / Our Lady of Guadalupe votive candle, acne ointment. I took a seat at a table. A table amid tile. I took out a pen and notebook with the intention of taking notes, wrote on the top of the first page, *McDonald's,* then crossed it out and wrote the plural possessive, *McDonalds',* then looked at the logo by the cash registers and crossed that out and wrote singularly again on the third line, *McDonald's,* put the notebook back in my coat.

It was exactly as I'd imagined it, which is to say exactly as I hadn't imagined it because I'd been imagining something imaginary to begin with—all down that sorry drain. Mopswishes, mopswishes on the floor, the fins of the mop, the mop's knotted tentacles swish across the floor. A golden-arched pyramid—a sandwichboard—cautioning "Slippery When Wet," and the sexual jokes that occasions, then that other phrase comes to mind, "on the clock," and there's a clock there, ticking shifts above the citations and mugshots: Employee of the Month wanted for armed robbery, non-support. Restroom coed but being cleaned, restroom coed but out of order.

Burger culled from asphalt, results in pothole. L(ettuce), t(omato), o(nion), mushroomcloud of sodafoam. I can make a noose with three straws, I can make a noose from two. A thirty minute seating limit, regularly enforced: a customer changing his seat every thirty minutes would take exactly how long to have occupied every seat (whatever's in that booth doesn't have to be homeless)?

Microphones foaming interjacent to the registers. Everything on the dollar menu costs a dollar. A dollar never includes tax. $1.08. $2.15. $3.23. $4.30 $5.38 $6.45. I was no longer so hungry, predictably. Thirst was more difficult. No soda would have been sufficiently large or sufficiently small. I had a medium thirst, a mediocre thirst. Only mediocrity would suffice and so becomes mediocre, preservative. A medium ensued. I sat, watched, listened. Big black and hispanic kids drinking blackcolored and hispaniccolored sodas. Fat old white man eating burger. The woman, his wife. Mashing pills into ketchup for fries. The climatized cold. The hard silence. A silence with edges. Open carton.

Flip up top. Chew pen turning tongue graveyard dark. The old man drooled above his seconds. Wife still finishing her first. Big burgers for those bloodless bodies! Those big big big big burgers! (No more writing, nothing more intelligent than that.)

THE COLLEGE BOROUGH

I helped build the Flatiron Building, though I've never been to New York—though Dem and I had never been before indulging our daughter Veri's desire to visit New York University—on my one week off this year and Veri's junior year springbreak—despite our hope that she, our only child, would choose to stay in-state.

The decision is hers—but we keep telling her, In-state was good enough for us.

After all, that's where we met.

Dem and I had four classes together prior to applying to Professor Greener's workshop—it was competitive certainly, but he accepted us both for what reasons we years ago came to terms with—this in the days when Dem was still doing poetry, not yet motherhood and the career of a freelance interior designer, the days when I was writing fiction as if literature were life.

And here was Veri, rebelling against our rebellion—she was bent on studying some profane concatenation of finance and psychology—she wanted to be employable, while all I wanted was to avoid the Flatiron.

And because I did, I insisted we do everything downtown: we'd sleep downtown at the Wall Street W (the hotel I'm writing from now, by midnight on W stationery with a W pen), we'd eat downtown (Dem an unreconstructed gastrophile when traveling, a compulsive cuisiniste who keeps files on restaurants, .docs and .xls spreadsheets of what dishes and deals can be had on what days where)—we'd tour and enjoy exclusively downtown: historic-districting around Trinity Church, the Exchange, the new Trade Center being built, going up slowly, slowly, after a decade of stagnancy, SoHo art galleries and Village bebop she'bam clubs (Dem had downloaded discount admissions), struggling improvisational comedy cellars (she'd scanned vouchers for three late sets free), and, Wednesday, if we can fit it in, one or two interactive museums.

Downtown's also where the school is, or rather *the school is downtown,* having taken everything over. The streets are the classrooms not in some ridiculously wistful sense but legitimately, or rather illegitimately—privately owned, zoned for children only.

Beat, footsore, inadequately caffeinated, Dem and I stood with our daughter at the front of the tour group led by a girl named like a corruption of a Dutch cheese—Goudla? Dougla? this cheerfully chubby checker of any survey's Pacific Islander box, majoring in—I wasn't paying attention—let's say postcolonial beading or basketry as therapy. She was very kind to Veri, very patient and always touching—Dem and even me, with a bit to the cuticle fingernail graze of my elbow, a hennaed palm to my shoulder, tender but then she'd think nothing of reaching out with a surprisingly firm grip and turning Veri's head to direct her attention: there the library, there the center for university life, here the freshman dorms (where you'll be living next year—what a presumptuous girl) . . .

I told Dem I wasn't impressed and she shushed me but I could tell from the side of her smile, she agreed. I'm saying the physical plant wasn't much. Prefab. Incapacitated by its overcapacity. Smogged. Now I know no city can contain all the amenities you'd find at a place like our alma mater. A city university just doesn't have the space, no matter how big the endowment, no matter what sums of R&D cash are banking around—Manhattan Island is only so large and it's telling that about half of its lower half is landfill. Back home we have more chlorinated pools, more recreation facilities with more stationary bikes and stairmasters, treadmills and the latest in weight machinery—hell, we even have the Flatiron, if you want to forgo the elevators and walk up it—the Fauxiron, Professor Greener once called it, whose roof I laid about twenty years ago, with Veri turning 18 this September.

I did a fine job on that building, finer workmanship than anything we saw on our tour save for a few of the older buildings—I'm talking the stolid stuff actually of the 1900s, those tiles and carvings from when we still cared about craft, those noble columns and colonnades and ornamental gutters—all the fineries I learned to duplicate, the techniques that usurped my writing to give me a destiny with salary and benefits.

You want Peterson's Roofing to do up your house, but first you want to looksee our standard? Go down to auxiliary field #3—incongruous, isn't it? insane, perhaps? jutting from amidst sports pitch and prairie, a skyscraper visible from the Mississippi, as the meeker, more Mormon guides claim when you take the tour of that campus. That slight wedge of trouble that has us wedged south of City Hall, that was Dem, that was me—clients call impressed, I do well for myself. Veri would thrive, twenty floors below that turbid eclipsing—1,750 miles away from 175 Fifth Avenue.

Professor Maury Greener was invited out to our flyover square state to be Writer in Residence for the 1992–1993 academic year on the merit of his recently published and only book, a novel about its author's formative years so searing, so bridgeandtunnelburning and explicitly realistic that we couldn't resist ravishing it for autobiographical fact (an interpretive approach that Greener both practiced and abhorred). So art reconstitutes biography—or better, biography like iron can make art like steel, but then the art can be heated again and the iron reseparated, the biography flowing molten all on its own—what a significant simile! such a suitable image! He—like his hero who shared his initials, height, weight, eye and hair color, wardrobe preference for wry denims, and predilection for deli—was born on the Brooklyn-Queens border, at the conjunction of those two potent, across-the-water boroughs so fetishized for having provided the nativity of so much authentic, impactful culture of the century past: Irish, Italian, Jewish, and he was the lattermost, he wouldn't let you forget it. Greener was the first Jew I ever met. Now I was a student of literature, not a student of the study of literature but of the making of literature (already there was the vocational calling: the desire to be trained to task, *to do, to make*), and though I was a voracious reader of the right writers—the lustier ethnics, the WASP authoritarians—practically speaking, my experience was nil. Jews were in the Bible, they were of the Bible. They weren't on my TV or in the movies I borrowed, but they made the TV and movies. I didn't expect him to have horns or anything—it was Dem's family (typically exasperating inlaws, but also bison ranchers) who'd passed along that stereotype and when Dem mentioned it to me after reading up on Greener before he arrived, I immediately imagined a man with airhorns, or megaphones, grown out of his head—and it wasn't like I was expecting a version of Shylock or Fagin, but I was not prepared for the irony, that fuck you and fuck your mother cynicism. This was because—memoir, self-writing again—he was raised without a father and had to toughen up fast. He had to learn—he taught himself, as his protagonist, M. Groonik, had taught himself—how to fight, how to stand up for what was his. What was his was Stuyvesant, followed by climbing the Ivy, uptown—rungs above the college Veri and Dem and I were touring, eons—humanities educationwise—beyond our own peonic undergraduate and graduate careers. And of course he had his book, which followed this titular Groonik, "amateur erector *cum* semiprofessional ventilation inspector," through myriad ménages à trois and quatre in downtown New York of the mid-1980s. What that book earned him: low advance on low sales, hysterical acclaim, and, once remaindered, once out of print, this sinecure stint in the provinces teaching us hicks *to rite good.*

It seems that the '80s—the decade of my adolescence spent lurching dazed between milking and collecting eggs at my parents' dairy farm and videogaming after homework—was the last tolerable decade in New York, despite the city going broke, despite the crime: it was Greener, who had eight years on me, who taught me to qualify. For him it was the decade of punk rock, hip hop, rap, graffiti as art, heroin and coke, a scene where everyone became millionaires at their mixed media before dying of AIDS or, as Greener wrote, "wrote excessive books about excess that were never excessively read" (though, he once recommended, the hardcovers' dustjackets were useful for cutting up lines)—the last decade before the encroachment of the rest of the country, before the suburbs moved into the urbis. All that pseudoculture that Greener hated: the chainstores, the megamalls, the ATMized shopfronts unmanned but anyway lit and heated and airconditioned 24/7/365—he hadn't been around any of that before it began coming to New York (downtown definitely has all the familiar logos by now), and just when it came he decamped to its source. He came to our state, our city, our cow college town—the world capital of bad depressing homogenous capital. We had—we still have, unupdated, unredone—an airport, then a strip of consumer options, then, up the hill, the College on the Hill and, when he first arrived, his second night with us—arrived unaccompanied at 35, balding and fattened like a species of livestock new to us who knew our livestock, but still recognizable as ready for slaughter—he invited Dem and me out to dinner along with a half dozen fellow students, but not because he wanted to bond.

He said, Don't think I want to bond, it's just that your girlfriend's too pretty, which for him passed for a compliment.

He stood us a round of dollar margaritas.

I didn't have the heart to tell him, *my fiancée* (that character still sounded too foreign).

All throughout dinner we were introduced to that hilariously raw style of metro complaint, the perpetual bitching of the provincial Manhattanite: could the food be any worse? could the service be any worse? could the fluorescents be more industrially fierce? which were cornier, the corn tortillas or the restaurant's muzak and decor (the decorations were stapled sombreros and hefty husks of lacquered maize, a burro mural in dishwater pastels below dishsized speakers blatting juvescent pop top-40)? could the conversation at the surrounding tables be any stupider? could the people tabled around him be any stupider? He was caustic. Could he get a new knife? He'd drunkenly clunked his last to the floor.

The food was nominally Mexican (his request)—did we take him to Taco John's or Casa Agave? I'm not sure which chains we had then—pre-Chi-Chi's, ante-Chipotle—Chili's?

About as Mexican as Hitler, he said, As Mexican as spätzle, he said, then, after the flan, wiped his mouth with the zarape that served as tablecloth and said:

Here's your first assignment.

And then took a shot of tequila and said, Margarine-flavored tequila.

For our virgin workshop in this burg, I want you to write

a story about our dinner tonight, but make me out to be the biggest asshole possible—I want to be fictionalized, hyper-fictionalized, let your imagination graze free on the range—have me robbing this joint, have me taking a shit in the rice and beans, out me as this pretentious pinko kikeabilly snob, though still deigning to rape your wives, he looked at Dem then looked at me, winked.

Hand that in, he said, or else.

Or else?

(It was like the entire waitstaff asked that too.)

Bring me anything you want.

Staggering out of the restaurant he was slurring, But I'll only read a story if it's finished.

The first story I brought Greener was my own original creation I barely remember save that it involved a young man who went away to war—which war? did I specify which or even have a certain war in mind? who came home with medals bandaging his wounds to find some things different, not drastically different, just slightly different, like his wife has a name that sounds like her old name or what he thought her old name was, or his daughter's just as beautiful as he'd remembered but instead of having green eyes and blond hair she has blue eyes and brown hair and this destabilizes him, this youthful veteran, who begins behaving differently himself, indulging in violent outbursts he and everyone around him regard as wholly uncharacteristic (unable to give this unrecognizable family affection or hold down a job, he blots his days trying to throttle a motorbike engine)—the reader has to wonder how sane he is and, if he's not sane, how that loss of sanity will end: with murdering his family? with murdering himself (the vet was based partially on my grandfather, WWII, partially on my father,

Vietnam—I've never served and that and the double models for the protag were probably why I kept the exact date and location of the conflict vague, though current events conspired to turn a few references Arab)?

Greener didn't like it, he didn't like: fiction about war, fiction about animals and farming (the ancient pastoral was fine but the modern rural, verboten), fiction about or narrated by children (who were the same as animals to him). Essentially he didn't like any writing by anyone living not him—here was a man at war with himself—though he did grudge me praise for the second story I gave him, which was the purposefully stilted, nearly dialogueless telling of an English professor, an expert at translating anacreontics, visiting this college far out in the stix to deliver a paper at a conference, fumbling through his presentation, stumbling into an unrecommended, ostensibly Vietnamese frytrap and getting so drunk at its incongruously tikified bar that he falls asleep on his stool and has to be woken and driven home by a waitressing doctoral student he offers "to put in a story"—or was it "to write into the next novel"?—if she sleeps with him, but she doesn't and instead leaves him sprawled in the rear lot of his motel, where delirious through the night he apostrophizes squirting skunks, revived only when he's hit in the head by the proprietor's newspaper delivery, that local paper Greener refused to read (incidentally the only paper that pubbed a positive obituary).

Apparently no other student had taken Greener up on his suggestion to turn him into lit and, when he cornered me after that inaugural class that left approximately half the roster in tears—its surprise subject was how if you intended to succeed as a writer it was necessary to move to New York—I could tell he was struggling with a reaction: whether to treat me like a fool for taking him so seriously, or to treat me like a prick for taking him so seriously (Greener was very attuned to prickishness, and to pretension, except in himself, except in his description of "a city so personal, it's as if it existed solely in dialogue").

Your traducing of me, he said, it's salvageable.

It is?

More so than most of the crap getting published.

He waited for a lesson in timing.

Then said, Which isn't saying much.

Greener turned to erase from the blackboard the map he'd scribbled, not showing but telling the locations of the better bookmarts of Manhattan (ten of which, Dem tells me, have since closed), then had me accompany him to his office and then, following farther—out.

He'd been in town—what? two weeks at that point? Calendrically it was still late summer, Indian summer, but, like the Indians, faded, failed. No one had welcomed him, I don't mean officially—the English department assisterati had requisitioned an ID card, dealt with the bursar in the matter of his tax forms, dealt with housing's sophomoric supernumeraries in the matter of his housing—I mean, by his own slyly pathetic admission, no one had just casually shown him around, given him the gossipy lay: what Dem and I and Veri were getting at NYU—e.g. this is the library, where you can basically make camp with an open fire and live in the stacks (Greener's class spent most of the fall doing that), the maths and sciences department, art, architecture, & design, journalism school, law school, center for experimental veterinary medicine. Greener was shocked by this greeting, honestly shocked, though what he interpreted as dereliction was merely the native reserve. Teaching being such a social activity—professors all day interacting, during office hours, in the hallways and restrooms with whomever they came across—that when their classes were over, they went home to stay home. They nested, our school mascot being an indigenously endangered nestbuilding bird. They projected documentaries and Scrabbled, chefed around elaborately, identified hobbies, attempted a baby. Certainly the school hadn't hired Greener only to ridicule him (they were pleased to have a minority: not someone Semitic, but someone who'd once been reviewed), certainly his agent hadn't arranged this appointment expressly to ruin him, as he maintained—though that suspicion, maybe, that paranoid loneliness revealed in his rage (what's the administration doing on weekend nights more entertaining than entertaining me? how many cold Sundays can I spend jerkingoff to the Hudson?), was why we, the two of us, were walking, or maybe it was that he wanted to use me to get closer to Dem, who'd returned to our apartment from workshop to dry her eyes and dry our laundry. Other faculty had tried to get to her before: Horniak, Rutter, and BJ, her poetry thesis adviser, whose plywood cubicle was adjacent to Greener's. Whenever he wasn't meeting with a female student, he, BJ—that bald bold unit postured like an italicized questionmark—was seated in front of the computer the school had just given him, trying to figure out which slot the discs went in, grouching that his monitor was busted when it wasn't plugged in.

I invoke this confusion to remind that when Greener was in residence, daily web use—campuswide internet access—was still a decade away. If our alma mater would've imported him just after the millennium, who knows if he would've felt so forsaken? who knows if he would've even dreamed of this gest?

As we roamed upper quad to lower, Greener became, by steps, progressively glummer until he was saying, You want to know the truth? New York's flunked me. Why else am I here? I've been suspended, I've been expelled.

I said, You seem to be doing OK.

Not compared to how I'd be doing if publishing weren't over, with the money gone and editors not editing, my generation's screwed—we're not the immigrant experience, we're not the assimilation experience—we're the first nothing generation, we've got nothing to write about and no one to read it, everyone too busy getting technologized, too harried with degrees.

Greener paused.

The conversation had taken an unpromising path. And we had too—leading down the hill to the labs.

Still we're better off than you are, he said—before you or your girl would even belong to a generation, you'd have to intern in midtown, where generations matter.

You're being unfair, I said, they matter here—your lineages and pedigrees—much more than on the coasts with all that transience.

I bummed a cigarette off him. Because he smoked, I smoked too.

I said, My family settled here before statehood—did I tell you I'm 1/16th Sioux?

He said, Intro to Identity. Multiculti Polyethnic 101. My parents survived Europe just so I'd write about it, they survived Europe just so I wouldn't.

Greener was the type who'd give you a cig but not a light.

I said, I was born here, completed every school here, Future Farmers of America central district secretary, which might not mean a lot to you but.

Greener interrupted to ask, What conceivably could have made you a writer?

The prairie grasses, the wheaty wilds, the good solid old-style people.

Bullshit.

Bullshit's a valuable fertilizer.

We'd walked into an unfertile field. A disused roughly triangular or sideways conical in its footprint pitch at the ragged edge of campus, which the baseball team—*Ra, Ra, Bara Cara, Hep Hep, Don't You Dare-A*—had used for practice before the new stadium was built.

A pitch outgrown with weed, rutted with deep mud troughs where the dean's tractor had rusted. Haybales, scattered silage troughs, hose. A pecked senseless scarecrow, straw packed into the uniform of last season's starting pitcher from a rival team one state over.

Greener and I stood next to each other along the lip of the outfield, dividing what was collegiate from pure nature.

He asked to feel my hands.

When we clocked in for the next week's workshop, a group of sincere and avidly morose shufflers, the room door had a slice of notepaper taped to its window at a reckless angle, *pat will bring you down to the field*—the handwriting that schoolboyish amalgamation of broad block and cramped cursive we'd become pros at deciphering—as for Pat, that's still me, and though Greener hadn't cleared this responsibility with me in advance, I led.

Trust me. Mind the foul lines. This way toward the margin. Rounding third base, second base, first.

Incredulous backpackers with mss., citrus pop going flat in our canteens.

We were twelve in that class assembled on a cooling day down at the rubbled heel of the pasture.

I was going to give a speech, Greener said.

But I won't.

He was standing on a haybale atop the pitcher's mound, then realized it was teetering shaky and stepped down to what remained of the dirt, a curveball's slogged mire.

Can everyone hear me?

He rocked for warmth—his suede breaker too light, it was just for style—clapped frayed Knicks cap over his ears, noosed tighter the unraveling knit scarf.

People are going to say I was homesick, he said, but that's just not true. Let me dispel. Allow me my disabuse. It's just that I can't in any way intuit how you all can write out here, with so much air and sky, with such openness, no disruptions, no disturbances.

Chiefly, nothing to compel ambition.

No opposition, no shadow, no shade for your toil.

We had no notion what he was saying.

Here, and he dug a sneaker toe into earth, we're going to build a sanctuary, a monument to our own publishability. Can everyone hear me? How many of you have been to the city?

The answers were: we all could hear him and only one or two warily raised hands—Rog and Bau, who'd won partial scholarships to a summer writing program (indeed at the very school I'm checking out).

On this pyramidal plot, he said, on this decaying diamond, we're going to make ourselves a culture—just for us and for whoever might suffer this school after, so that they might know what it's like to live in a culture, what it's like to be in a culture, to have culture, not just this organized sports frattery and hayseed academe.

In the grass grown wild at his feet was a shovel, a rusticated bluefaced tool he bent to and picked up and kicked into earth, breaking ground.

Broadway's a difficult street, it's touchy, temperamental,

a diva—Greener tossing a shovelful of soil into the wind, the silty loam gusting back into his face and so he stalled, not to brush but to swallow—Broadway's historic, taking time to find its bearings.

Dig deep into your thesauri for this: *slithery, serpentine, anguiform* even: you see that in how it winds up from the Battery and Wall Street (Greener dramatizing by digging the path with the shovel from his groundbreaking up toward the mound), how it swerves shyly to avoid Washington Square (he reached to a back pocket for a pair of mittens, dropped them), then suddenly cuts off (he took off his cap), at Union Square (dropped the cap), in preparation for its regeneration, regrowing itself in realignment when it crosses Fifth Avenue (the perimeter of the mound itself heading toward the bale), taking the central action of town and reorienting it to the westside.

That's where downtown grew up—on the westside—is this making sense?

We nodded.

Don't forget I'm speaking as a pedestrian, as a weekend cartographer in comfortable shoes—I was walking you through the thoroughfare north, though the traffic, I have to say, flows south.

Nodding.

But we're particularly concerned with that intersection, where Broadway walks all over Fifth—one to become the snobby society money boulevard, that ignorant lilywhite stretch, the other to become that concourse of dirty miscegenation, a corridor potholed, poorly sidewalked and stuck with gums, obscurely tenanted—Broadway, the broad way, the wrecked wide and embracing inclusive anything goes way, the name almost unpacks itself.

A breeze blew in, autumn hinting at winter.

We shivered.

And we're going to remake that here, he said, rather its landmark.

His hands described a structure in air, cold lines of cold air.

From now on all classes will be held out here under the clouds, both semesters regardless of weather—I've managed to persuade the school to approve our use of this field.

There will be a dress code.

He was calibrating, calculating.

There will be forms to sign, insurance waivers.

He steeled himself to say, You won't be handing in writing for the rest of the year.

Which is how we began building, began rebuilding, the Flatiron. Built in 1902 and originally known as the Fuller Building—after the pioneer of the modern skyscraper and inventor of the system of "contracting," G. A. Fuller, *1851–†1900, whose firm went on to build Penn Station, Macy's Department Store, the Plaza Hotel, and the original New York Times Building, all of which are too uptown for our itinerary—the Flatiron was "the first great skyscraper in New York," though it was "built in the style of Chicago" (its architect was a Chicagoan called Burnham)—all this according to the infopacket Greener passed around along with photocopies of the original blueprints illegally reproduced from the archives of the New York Historical Society (an exgirlfriend librarianed there, he'd said, Greener was always mentioning exgirlfriends—one who'd starred in a blaxploitation flick he forbade us from mentioning, another who'd had her own let's meet our panel of nymphomaniacal nannies talkshow—I often had the feeling he'd come out to our crop only to avoid the famous feminine back east).

Also included in the packet were photos: souvenir posters and postcards, antique panoramic exposures and aerial snaps, in color and, why not, black & white (which Greener declared the only colors worth building for). The building looks different in every shot. Seen from the front it resembles a single column, as upright as Classicism, as upright as Neoclassicism, a spine straight up and down, but seen from the side it's a monstrous wall, like a cursorless screen, or that virtually blank page that'd directed us down to its rising. Greener quoted numerous writers—of fiction and poetry of the period of the building's initial erection—comparing that frontview to a steamship steaming its prow up the avenues, and the sideviews, both starboard and port, to a sailboat's sail or the blade of a knife—Greener remarking, however, that since it was built on an island, was built on a traffic island, if the building was a boat, it was beached. Though the Flatiron was among the first genuine skyscrapers to be constructed of steel—previously steel wasn't considered entirely reliable, its properties not yet understood—it didn't get its name from the metal that made that material. Rather the name that branded the building and district as enduringly as the building itself branded the city, predates construction, deriving from a resemblance— evident to the nineteenth century, aka the century Greener thought we were from—between the Flatiron's future plot and a clothes iron. (I'm writing this not on the W's room's desk, which is filled with Veri's purse and cosmetics, but on the ironingboard retrieved from the closet, remembering Dem pressing our pleats, cooking soufflé buffets with truffles. Remembering myself walking fantasy crossroads with Greener, talking plans, talking tenants—Greener pointing out how the Flatiron separates downtown, which creates the art, from midtown, which rapaciously profits from it, how the building itself points north toward the agents and publishers, toward the magazines too, who'll be so interested in this project, they'll send photographers, glossy journalists with expense accounts equivalent to a year's pay for my freshman comp adjuncting—grandiosity!)

Beneath the Flatiron's fancy cladding, undergirding the swooping loops and oriels—the limestone base and glazed terra cotta facade are in no way loadbearing—is that metal, the steel, which was Rog Reardon's assignment. From that second week of class he began spending a lot of time at a foundry just outside town that was closed when the company that had owned it was bought by another company that was bought by another company that moved to Mexico. As the foundry had fired Rog's father and uncles, it was Rog's pleasure to rehire them and refire the works. These metalworkers, family and those unrelated but friends and acquaintances, were happy to be employed, less happy to be so on the condition that Rog apprentice as mill supervisor. But Rog proved adept, a swift learner. Greener, it should be understood, had a phenomenal sense for assignments, and besides the useful fortuity of Rog coming from a steel-making family, it also helped that the novel he'd been neglecting since junior year was imprecise about its narrator's identity, relationships, and ambitions, abstract in its philosophy, sloppy with flashback and dream, and what it needed, what Rog needed, was nothing more than dense hard verbs, relentlessly accurate adjectives, and the active immediacy of the present tense. By midterm, Rog had become an expert, rallying the townie workers to their largest job in decades. Today Mr. Reardon serves as foreman and half owner, with the university, of the foundry, and is arguably the best, most successful steelman in the state (his daughter—Raina? Raisa? has been in every one of Veri's classes through high school, though I don't know why they never got along—Veri says she's spoiled).

Moreton did the foundation work and now has a prospering cement business of his own out of the county seat (he also owns part interest in a quarry). He set our house and has become a good, thorough, methodical, even plodding man, which every time I bump into him—in line at the hardware emporia, at the gas stations by the Route 70 onramp—unsettles me, given that the problem with his writing was that it'd lacked what he now supplies so well: the groundsill, the footings, a bottom. He, a poet, used to be a sound guy, a line freak, just making weak beams of pretty and pretty shocking words to tickle the ear (he'd mix metaphors too), but there'd be no formal structure, no prosodic meter, just stray vowels and consonants, snippets he'd heard and read in Eagle Avenue cafés floating as moments—occasions—without anchor or ballast. Greener—I think, I have to think though he never said anything about his selections—intuited this and sent him delving into bedrock, wood pilings, concrete, rebar. This was his specialty, Greener's, countering a writer's faults—supposed faults because Greener had read only one submission by each student—with a physical, practical correction.

Sora, who'd overwrite and overcharacterize and overdetermine and overexplain and just spoonfeed you, the reader, everything—she'd tell you what clothes a character was wearing only when it had no bearing on her story, she'd cite exactly what kind of meals her villain was munching when it had precisely nothing to do with advancing her arc or deepening characterization (why should it matter that her Alaskan psychic lesbian spy preferred spotted jumpers belted with appliqué flowers, pink pigskin gloves, and purplestriped, kneehigh galoshes, a strict diet of turkey chili and fries?)—Greener, with his genius, turned her transparent, light and free and freely pertinent. He made her our glazier, and wouldn't you know it, she's become our own home's window woman, and is even developing an exclusive make of energysaving window that reduces heating costs, has a screen that can be raised only from the top sash as a child safety feature, and, I remember, Dem was just telling me—Dem's in touch with her from the gym and PTA—that it recently won some national design award. Congrats, Sora! Let's catch up sometime!

As Bau's poems were always scatological—clogged to their brims with sex, piss, and shit—Greener, as if imparting a moral lesson, put him on plumbing, while Lo—whose poems and ersatz fairy and folktales, in contemporary settings, were so precious and vapidly schematic—was assigned to electrical. Of course they're married now, Bau and Lo, and in business together and, though Dem and I don't get together with them more than once a year since they transferred west to tend to Lo's mother when she stroked herself into dementia, we still think of them often and fondly. Two kids, boys: Maury, a hapless pick, after the prof, and don't quote me on this, Billy Jr.

As for Dem, to Greener's mind—and to ours as well, though it took time and the necessity of dual incomes for us to countenance this—her poems were all surface gaiety, superficially stunning in their detail but emotionally empty: no amount of technique, and Dem had tons, could compensate for her being so private and timid, withdrawn. But how to teach emotion? How to teach the turning of the insides out? Greener had a solution (to get inside her he had to extrovert her first, that was my reaction). He put her in charge of interior decoration, her brief being not to duplicate the interior of the building as it was at the time of its construction—we weren't getting into any period furniture, anyway how to find such records, if there were any such records—neither to duplicate the interior at present, or at the present of the century's turn, rather to create a new interior, "one conducive," Greener handwrote in a memo Dem typed for herself on a computer afforded her by the engineering department (its only cooperation), "to conducting literature classes & writing workshops &c."

"Show me comfort."

"Make for me an ideal."

Being the only position with any modicum of creative control, this was a major honor and Dem knew it but also knew it meant that she and Greener would be spending hours of overtime together, alone, poring over that ratty portfolio she hauled to the site daily—crammed with paint swatches (the multiple offs: the laces, pearls, ivoire), fabric samples (tanned durables), clippings of any pattern wallpaper that caught fancy—though he tried to kiss her only once.

It was then—Dem coming home blushing sunset—that I flipped, showed up on the lawn of his faculty bungalow an hour later, screaming into the dark, Come on out, motherfucker, I will scalp you of your fucking testicles, and out Greener came in his tightywhities with a red, yellow, and green stoplight plaid robe blown loosely around him, wielding only a scroll of blueprints like a scopic spear, saying, That's right, Pat, that's what's wrong with your work—it's all impulse, it's all energy, it's good impulse, sure, it's good energy, fine, the right true spirit, but still that's not enough, it goes nowhere, you have nothing planned (waving the cyanotypes into blackness), nothing kept in reserve (stamping his feet, one bare, the other fuzzy, sheepishly slippered).

What the hell's wrong with my work?

What were you going to do, kill me? What were you thinking?

I don't know.

Bingo. You have no forethought—you just start a sentence without knowing how it ends, without knowing where or when it ends. Capital letter, then you skimp on anything that comes before the closing punctuation—if there's any punctuation.

I was panting, snuffle, mucus.

Put commas between your instincts, parse reflexes into clauses—the same goes for your personal life.

I attended this lecture—I always had perfect attendance.

So I made a move on Dem—so what? she rebuffed me. You're too much the idiot to recognize what's essential: she doesn't want me, she wants you.

That's what she said.

He scowled

I said, She told me not to do this—she said if I came over here I couldn't ever come home.

Pat, you need to calm, keep the passions controlled—why else did I make you my roofer?

Greener shambled to the door of his tickytacky ramshackler, held it open for me.

Give Dem time to chill—she'll take you back in the morning.

How sorry is it that writing about that evening with Greener is no easier now than it was then—years ago, the summer after that evening, when the media called? Predictably late. Nonfiction, they asked for. Journalism, they demanded. Editors, installed floors above realism, interested not in a crew of yokels and their architectural success, but in sensationalizing a former peer's failure. Dem was furious I'd even considered their offers—that spat ruined our honeymoon, Canada—though it's not like I would've been able to complete any "article," any "piece." I declined by maintaining I was too biased by hurt, but, full disclosure: I couldn't write anymore, I wasn't a writer.

I'd never been inside Greener's bungalow before and I didn't want to be there then—I wanted to demolish him, but I'd never been in a home so depressing. Not even those small poor places Dem and I would rent when Dem was still diligently sewing and gluing her verses together by day and then, once she had a job too and we were less poor, by night—not even that condemned chapel that leaked, or that dingy duplex downwind from the rendering plant I patched up nice but the toxic mold mucked in just when Veri was born—not even those could compare.

Greener had no furniture, no possessions. He had only this expression: mad, insomniac, grim.

He didn't even have any literature on the nonexistent shelves, just how-to's piled on the floor, stacked in the cupboards and pantry.

No manuscripts in the microwave unplugged, just diagrams, bank statements.

I've sold everything I shipped out with, he said. School's only put up $100K, I'm funding the rest.

From your royalties? from your foreign rights and options?

By the grace of my mother's estate and with loans, I'm buying myself a borough.

You're in debt?

And did I mention my publisher rejected my new book last week? More of the same, they said.

More of what?

It's a novel that revises my previous novel—do you honestly care?

Why do this to yourself?

I'm a teacher, I'm teaching.

We're learning (I winced from my lameness).

And I'm going for broke on your education—though it's incredible what you can get done with free labor.

You're counting on this class to support your retirement?

(A jest as uncomfortable as lounging on his shack's sloppy planks.)

The end of the semester's the end of me.

And then what?

Rewhiskeying my mason jar, lighting two Camels, handing me one   And then we'd better be finished.

Tub was the only one of our class to leave town, the county, the state (as far as Dem and I are aware). He was always smart, too smart to be a writer it occasionally felt, Tub the brainiac always so analytical, so literal. I knew him, as I knew most of my fellow classmates, from prior workshops—those with hypertext experimentalist Grazinski, whose avant lacked only a garde, those immersed in the bucolic bardics of BJ, whose eclogues insisted on rhyme—and so I knew that if a character in some student's story went somewhere, like New York City, say, on a certain date at a certain time, Tub would research that date and time and quiz the author on trivia like the weather (drizzle in the morning? leading to an afternoon of scattered thunder?), or how might your character react to the news that the Monday before the Jets holocausted the Eagles? or that two girls, braided black twins, died in a house fire in Harlem? He was a stickler, a looming, hovering pain, so Greener, surprise, surprise, promoted him to contractor (elevating Greener, I guess, to the role of contractor's contractor).

Tub kept us on time, managed the workflows, made sure everybody made their right contributions in the right order and that when it was too early to do the plumbing or electric, for example, Bau and Lo weren't allowed to just hump away at the edge of the lot—the field had been referred to as "the lot," or "the site," then gradually Greener's appellation spread, I spread it: "the college borough"—but were instead redirected to help with unloading trucks, or putting up scaffolding, aiding—meaning following and learning from—Mesh and the region's most skilled masons on their facadework. (Mesh was assigned the facade, that intricate, fripperant facade, only because the surfaces of his literary work were so terribly transpicuous, so banally boring—simple declaratives rife with simple vocabulary. Plain. Unadorned. Also it'd be shabby not to note that at this juncture, the unions—Locals 5, 15, 35, and 86—were pitching in for nothing, in a recruitment initiative, whenever they had shifts to spare.)

Tub himself wasn't exempt from this diversification and though his primary talent was obviously organizational—he was a frail, wan guy—Greener insisted that he assist on the grunt jobs too, and so not only did he learn, as we all learned, something of every discipline, he also built up his chest and arms and successfully overcame chronic asthma. And Greener, it should be said, wasn't exempt either: out straining among the elements, stooped for lift over pallets, it was as if he too would be receiving a grade. A fountain of sweat. Tanned in even his creases. He never cleaned his workboots or helmet. He looked wonderful (no, no: he looked like he was wonderfully dying).

It was late in the afternoon, about an hour after we'd returned to the hotel from the NYU tour, in the middle of the brief nap we'd scheduled before beginning to plan which of Dem's tapas reservations to honor—

My phone rang a strange (212) number, but I answered it

anyway, figuring it was the airline or an autoconfirmation of our visit tomorrow early to Liberty Island.

It's Tub, he said, Tub Deminty—why didn't you tell me you two were in town?

How did you know?

Reardon emailed with your number, it's been forever, I hope you're not avoiding me.

It's not you I'm avoiding, I thought but only repeated, Damn straight, forever.

And I'm told you have a girl doing the rounds of our fair borough's higher ed?

You're on top of it.

Dem sat up in bed.

I know this is rushed, but will you make time for me tonight? I fly tomorrow for Frankfurt.

Dem cocked an ear.

I'll get you tickets to *Willies,* that play that just won the Pulitzer—I'm friendly with the producers. Three tickets at Will Call (I have a meeting)—you'll see the show then after we'll eat, when the restaurants aren't so crowded. Sound good? You in the mood for Turkish?

Dem snatched the phone from me, yelled, Have you heard of this taverna on East 66th?

And hello to you too—Tub had heard of it. He said that tables were scarce but he'd try. If that was a bust, he knew an exquisite rawfood trattoria.

He'd be the man with the olive umbrella, waiting just up the block from the theater.

Tub—why had I wanted to steer clear of The Tub, who used to write minuscule essays of sublime erudition but of no argument, no sway or opinion, just compressed paragraphicules of unremitting fact? Did I think he'd outgrown me, transcended our Midwestern muddle, advantaging his expertise, relocating to New York to do architecture, still scrupulously unmarried, still no children, if I had to pry gay, on staff at the Landmarks Commission—impeccably preserved himself—responsible for approving all reconstructions and refurbishments, all additions and subtractions, to the city's historic buildings?

Nope, it wasn't anything that petty, nothing that begrudging—it didn't pique that he was the only one of us who'd published (though it was only an academic monograph on the history of brick)—no, my problem, getting down to street level, was just that he was the closest of our classmates to the edifice itself, a New Yorker who probably passed that prototype daily and was probably solely responsible for its welfare. How could he take that? how lucky can you get with your education?

Now just like the professionals we become after we graduate aren't constructed merely from our student experiences, literature isn't built merely of words—instead both require an extra material, whatever quantity of indefinable spirit that sent Tub to parts east, me up to the roof, and Dem to designing and decorating even after, especially after, what happened with Greener.

A writer, or a couple of exwriters, staying in this city at the W Hotel, might express their room's bed and chair and desk by just repeating the words *bed* and *chair* and *desk*— while any deepening of a reader's appreciation would depend on deepening the descriptions.

Would depend on, inspiration.

Following Greener, however, Dem preferred to choose a room's furnishings rather than choose the verbiage that furnished their details.

A writer can write "the room had a couch," or a writer can just give up writing, go out and drag a couch back into the room, having selected the appropriate model—it's this total specificity, this absolute precision, that allowed Dem, having left the arts, to once again keep her exterior flawless and her interior private, her own.

By early evening, Dem had become particularly obsessed with the W's room's curtains—while I shaved twice, fussed with a suit, and pretended to worry about being late, this was her attempt to distract me.

On our way out she stopped at reception to ask, Where did you source it? that gorgeous microruffled white muslin?

The concierge didn't know but said he'd do research, And, Madam, you have excellent taste.

He was a boy with a face from home, which he bowed to his tie, to repolish his accent.

I piled the family into a taxi, instructing the driver—Iranian? Iraqi? allow me to claim I'm too bumpkiny for such distinctions—to head uptown, but to take the West Side Highway (I should've subwayed, though which train's a mystery).

Dem—vacillating between nervousness at traveling to an unknown, possibly even undatabased restaurant, and guilty joy at finally gaining the island's northern latitudes—suppressed those sentiments out of concern: she was staring out the window then canting back in my direction, fixing me with her big blue salty puddles.

Veri wasn't privy to any of this—didn't know about that past, not even rumor. Inevitably she knew I'd roofed that dilapidated campus building modeled on another dim building dimly in New York—but how was that remarkable when I'd also roofed her friends' houses, our neighbors', our own barn and stables and four-bedroom, five-bathroom mock Colonial Revival, Mesh's manse, and every home ever mortgaged by Bau and Lo from starter rancher to condo? She was gorging on the trailmix Dem passed her. She was very excited for her first Broadway show.

At Canal Street the darkling driver said, Too much the traffic is, an accident must be, as he swerved to continue north on—Bowery.

I asked, Can't I choose the route?

The cabbie said, Bowery is best.

My phone rang a txt from Tub, No Greek or Ital, Yes Tk meze korean bbq v. delish.

I return txted, Whever?

As the avenues split I cried, No, stop, but Dem turned to mouthbreathe, No, *you stop.*

Dad? Veri said.

Sirs? said the cabbie.

Enough, Dem said, you're a man.

I slouched, resigned—I'm the roofer.

The avenue gave way to Park.

Tub wasn't there at the end, I mean the very end.

He was away doing what Veri was doing now, checking out schools, for him architectural school, not just touring but having his interview, "his intellectual texts" (that was his terminology)—like pot or hallucinogens—a twenty-something hobby.

Not just him, nobody was there at the finish—they were all in their dorms, cramming the New York City building code of the era, or out at the library studying the Beaux-Arts.

Ultimately there was just me.

The roof is, by default, the last.

Can't build the ceiling before the floor.

I went up after a fierce spring storm to check the coping—the balustrades, that overbearing cornice (unnerving resemblance to Greener's chin)—ensure all my work had withstood its final exam.

Topside was wet, slick. Ponds sloshed across the verdigrine tar, drowning the ducts.

Greener stood, trembling.

We all knew he'd been living in the Fauxiron for a few weeks, but nobody had dared to say anything beyond, If you need a shower or are peckish, don't hesitate, drop by. Dem had outfitted him with a decent penthouse suite replete with foldout sofa, stocked minifridge, full bath, but mostly he slept—as evidenced by the Baby Ruth and straw wrappers, the Coke cans and bourbon fifths and butts and last week's bundled socks—in the halls or in random other studios. Or up on the roof come April and May, with the term almost over—he had no summer plans (he'd been using his rejected manuscript as pillow until, over springbreak, with us away at Dem's parents', he burnt it in his suite's trashcan to test the alarms, or so he'd told the authorities—the alarms worked, the sprinklers worked, did damage).

The taxi approached the intersection—I was sitting on its west side, was fated to that side.

On the roof I reached a hand out—reached a hand out the cab's window too—pointing a finger at the air.

The wind the smoothest traffic.

Dem held my knee and Veri, bright with recognizance, shouted, Hey, where are we?

The intersection of voids, the corner of nothing and nothing.

I turned to the rear window.

A laugh.

There it was in its rude sedate slant, there it was in its glory.

The height from which he jumped.

SENT

I. The Bed

Beds are made of trees, and coffins are beds with lids. Death is sleep without bottom. Its nature silent and consciousless and densely dark—

Imagine you are walking through a dream. But your dream is not just that, not just open. Your dream isn't just one big gray open scape of mist you can step into, you can walk anywhere through, stick a hand or arm or leg into and just wiggle anywhere, no.

There are obstructions, even here. This is a dream with obstructions.

And so it is real. So it is real life.

You are walking through the forest but you cannot walk straight, you have to walk where the forest says you can walk, around the trees that tell you Here and There and Here. If straight is your goal you will have to go crooked. If crooked is your goal you will have to aim crookeder. No, better a fairy should tell you, some sort of dryadish creature: *"If straight be your goal you must go crooked. If crooked be your path go forth and crook."*

Yes, fairy. Yes, cretin sprite.

I am a woodsman. A forester. No. You are a woodsman. You are a forester. No. Shake the tree. Uproot the roots. He, yes, *he* is a woodsman, he is a man in the woods. He is thick like wood and brown like wood and nothing about him is green. He has a bark beard. Knots for eyes and knots for ears and a knot for a mouth but while walking he is silent. His wife he has left behind in their hut. From there, noises. Their hut is made of trees, is made of tree, unwindowed. She lies on the ground expecting a child. This would be their first. New leaves, new leaf, a child shaped in lobes with a stem between the legs. She lies there in labor, lies on the earth belabored, olid and fat. She screams and screams and her eyes are angry. (He needs to move quickly.)

Fairies? *"You need to move quickly!"*

Thou spirits of lilim and such? *"Hurry, hurry fast!"*

He must build her a bed. He must build her a bed she can give birth in. And it must be built well so that the birth will be well. But he has to do this soon, has to rush.

His ax has a name but no one will know that name. That name is a secret unlike the name of his child that everyone will call him or her, he is expecting a Him. The axname is secret because that is the name he calls when he needs the ax's power. The ax was smelted especially for his father, with magical powers that his fathers believed in and that he, the child of his father, believes in occasionally. But he also wonders occasionally why an ax should have an axname like a child has a childname but the ax's name secret, and there is an unease in that wonder that he does not understand fully or want to. (Enough to know that the ax is sharp, though he's not sharpened it since he was married. Not a whet since he was wed. He has cut hairs with it, though, his, his wife's, he's cut with it the throats of hairs and the limbs of wild game and is not worried.)

The seed for the tree came on a whistling wind when God was new or the fathers were gods or when there wasn't much of a difference between them—it was blown in on the wind and then the wind stopped its whistling and there the seed fell and became planted with the force of its fall and was watered with raining. Weather, nothing more eternal than the weather. The woodsman was not a godtype, he couldn't have been one even if eternal. He was ugly and fat and short. "O God Above [but this was just a thing he said] I am ugly and fat and short of haft!

"But my ax is strong."

The tree grew to be an amalgam of trees. A composite of marbled meats thick and dark under a bark. When struck, splintering like a muscle stretched apart. As a tree it was the widest but most stunted like him so he chose it and cut it because it was like cutting himself, which is what a child will do, he will cut you. Imagine you chopped open a tree and inside was a very small tree. That is what it's like to be human. To be both conscious and conscious of one day not being—and so we seed another.

The tree—which had been rained upon by centuries, its shoot trampled by armies invading and the sport of the hunt, having shaded picnics with Mama and lovers around its expansive trunk graffitied with the endearments of pocket knives and quivering arrows—took only an afternoon in which to fall, after which the woodsman dragged it through the woods under the lush green eyes of its upright fellows, shedding leaves shaped like tears and hearts and leaves back to his hut where he left it in the clearing, just outside the door. He did not go in to greet his wife, the sounds of her shrieking told him she was still alive and had not birthed yet. He did not need to go in, did not need to hear her shriek, already knowing that all would be well, that all would be Malc: in the woods he'd buried a hunk of the dung he'd squatted for in the rough hole left by the uprooted tree, in order to propitiate (thank) the forest powers.

And though he did not believe in those woody powers anymore as his father had believed in them, and though he told himself that he often enough did not believe even in God anymore, still he squatted in pressure and heat and left in gratitude what he left—a stillborn blackish coil.

Then he made the bed.

But I should tell this story the way one should tell this story to someone who has never made a bed. When you tell this story to a fellow bedmaker you just say, *He made One!*

What did he do? he made a bed (not with sheets but

with wood and nails), what kind of bed? a big wood bed he nailed—nevermind how, you whose beds at home be unmade, nevermade. Nevermind the chop chopping, the lathe hump of knots to flatness and the plane, the planing. Nevermind those nails, which in days of yore my little squirty grandkids you had to make yourself, not buy, you couldn't buy them. He made the nails from out of dug earth, fingerdug—but there'd be no need to tell this to a nailmaker. Or to a fellow storyteller. Fill it in yourself.

There, the bed is done.

I will next explain its symbols.

"Please explain . . ."

To begin with the bed was built and was built plainly given the haste, and babies were birthed upon it, but then over the years in his rare eventide leisure the woodsman would carve into the bed, would make carvings into the footboard of the bed, and into the bed's headboard too, with that selfsame ax held nearer the blade and then his practiced knife.

On the footboard, the lions he carved represented the strength of lions. The four bedposts he topped with carvings of antlerlike crowns represented authority. Or they might have signified majesty instead, we're not sure and neither was he, guided by hand and whimsy. Yet again the entirety might only have represented "Representation."

On the footboard he carved swords and fearsome wings that might've been of eagles or ravens if they had to be of something, something flying and not abstract. And he carved lances and bound sheaves of wheat but perhaps it was not wheat because who could grind it? who could grind wood and taste of it and think, wheat? That would be magic! That is the magic of saying This is That, of saying Here is There but it's not *but it is,* and that is poetry, which is a kind of art!

The woodsman carved into the footboard's wood a shield and a helmet and a pike and a mace, he carved a wood wolf, he carved wolves, carved a wooden steer, a stag and lamb, antlers, antlers more and more ornate, a boar, a bear. This was all hopeful, this was wishful, in a sense—this heraldry coming before the family to be heralded was finished. The woodsman, late at night, unprepared for sleep, was inventing the insignia for his family before family he had, because one daughter is not a family and neither are two daughters, but three daughters like in the olden stories, one pretty, one smart, one stupid and plain, are a family and then a son, who ignored the bed because he was too busy building his own life—he was too busy building his own life plainly and then, once finished, decorating it with ornament: with children of his own, grandchildren of his own.

The woodsman's son never noticed the bed, being too occupied growing his fortune, taking ore from the mine he worked in and piling it up, ore into ingot, into a huge new house with vast windowed rooms and whitewashed cabinetry with a silver filigreed tea set including matching kettle and minuscule handled bathtub for cream and bronzepotted rubberplants that grew to outlandish heights and editions of books in foreign languages that were about sex but served their women readers morals at the end, and he only used his father's shack as a shed for his wife's pampered, preciously fed livestock and, subsequently, for his newly acquired telephone the elaborate size of the automobile just then being invented but an ocean away that no auto could cross.

And this son, who worked his way up through the mines from working down in one up to soon managing the one he used to work at, eventually had two sons of his own and the older son one day looked at the headboard of the bed they kept for the family's babies to sleep in and for the importuning use of visiting relations and guests, in the rarest moment of Sunday repose looking at his grandfather's carving on the bed's headboard of a man among trees and saying to himself then aloud and in quotes, "I see a man among the trees. My grandfather carved into this bedhead a scene of himself going out among the trees to cut one down to make of it the bed my father was born in. It is no more difficult than that, yet neither is my life. I have married well a landowner's daughter and, like my father before me, have worked in a mine and now manage the mine my father managed, my life has been work, not as much work as life had been for my father or grandfather, but it has been a success because of them, their sorrows."

His brother—who was younger, a redskinned diminutive regarded as unmarriageable, born late in their father's middle age—scoffed at what his brother had said and said instead, "You have no senses besides your eyes, brother! You're made entirely of surface! This carving our grandfather carved on the headboard of our father's bed quite obviously depicts the peasant or workingman imperiled in a forest of giants—in a forest of towering landowners and Titans of industry like your father-inlaw—and he, the symbolic proletarian, is dwarfed by them, in their shadow he is dwarfish and inconsequential. Indeed, this carving must represent to us the coming war where the poor who toil in the fields and in mines like ours will revolt against the rich who own the fields and mismanage the mines and after that war is ended no man will ever be lost in the woods of another's exploitation."

And then there was a war. And both brothers fought in it but on opposite sides, the older brother compelled to fight in time but the younger brother an eagerly early volunteer for the Revolution that came through their country like a flood and like fire. And though the older brother—that pressured conscript fighting on the side of the greedy landowners and factory management—died in combat with a bullet just a screaming kopek paid to one ear, the younger brother survived and was in his medaled survival happy to decamp to a smaller apartment when his family's house was nationalized by the State after that war of class struggle concluded.

And so leaving behind everything for the comfort of the State—the tables and chairs and loveseat for the State to relax in along with a footstool upon which the State could rest its feet if it would expropriate any feet—the brother wracked with considerable guilt took with him and his nursemaid wife only the bed that was soon to be their daughter's—their daughter who grew up tall and silently beautiful and unlike her mother, who was the daughter of a Revolutionary mine secretary, was very wellschooled, having been sent away to university in the capital city to study biology and squint around with microscopes but for only a year before she had to return home with another war, this time an international war beginning because it was time for her to get serious about the future of building her country and life, which meant marriage.

And she saw in the bed in her parents' house she returned to, the bed she'd almost forgotten from childhood, in its headboard carved with the scene of the man wandering alone amongst the wood trees at night—a symbol of sorts, though when she was younger she could not define it or untangle the meaning of her sadness. Her switching the radio off to better look at it long late at night, lying with her head of long straight brownblonde hair mussed against the foot of the bed in the style of its wavy grain, in her maturation seeing in the carving of the carverman lost amid the immense trunks of trees a symbol for, yes, that was it, *existenz* (the university had given her that foreign word as a dowry), for man's essential predicament in the universe, how we are lonely and lost to wander among trees so immense as to be incomprehensible around us, not sure how we got into the woods or how to get out of them if ever, and she saw that that carved man—she didn't know he might be the carver himself, her greatgrandfather—was actually all men and all women too, unfixed, inconstant, errant in nature just like the boy she flirted with declaimed: *"On the branch bare and lone / trembles the belated leaf,"* a young man who wrote her extensive letters though he lived just across the courtyard, who smoked cigarettes he rolled with great fast skill and drank deeply from a flask and scribbled his own poetry with jetliner imagery and attended the movies regularly (but he'd never hold her hand during the newsreels).

She married him when he came back from that next war alive, marrying him because just as the only expression of wood is in its carving into a thing, the only expression of love can be marriage. And if a man who should be dead lives, then when he comes back from his war wounded—even if wounded in only his youth—a monument should be erected to him. And there is no better monument than a child—not wood, not even granite.

She took the bed with them as a cradle, moving it into their apartment they were reassigned to on the outskirts of their city (the country's second city: this was the city of culture, not the city of business, though in truth neither could lay claim to either). An old inconvenient wooden bed hauled incongruously up to the eighteenth floor of a prefab prestressed panel tower above a playground poured to harden around a gnarled jungle gym and rusty teetertotter teetertottering, a shattered liter of milk frozen into a purple skating rink in the light waned through the birches—it was the oldest and, given years, only wooden thing in their apartment of metal things and, given another decade, plastic clothing and plastic plates and plastic bottles and plastic glasses.

But her daughter, her daughter of flesh and not of plastic, the daughter's daughter when she encountered the bed throughout her lazy childhood—sitting on its lapse as if a couch to watch across the armlengthwide apartment the television set no bigger than a keyhole—decided that its headboard depicted no symbols or representations at all, that there was at base nothing to that headboard's carving but a man standing in the woods, nothing but a man on one hand and the woods on the other and one was in the other and surrounded by it and that was the way it was and would be forever and nothing meant anything or could be signified. This was what she concluded—she who did not know trees, she who could not identify which trees if any in particular had been carved into the headboard's wood that was of a type she could not identify either. She stared at it inattentively over Tokyo cartoons about undersea robots dubbed into sibilant Slavics and would think only that it was nice, the bed, that it was nicely comforting but also old and disgusting and a disgrace to the new that could not be afforded or even enough manufactured in the days when she sat on it painting her toenails with seagreen and white housepaint, affectionate tokens from the building's manager who was infatuated with her and sat with her in silence watching her read her tricolor Femininka magazines and drinking with her tea with "cognac" (which he'd also brought, provenance uncertain).

Watching the television she would, when bored with the program or news, which was often because the programs were always boring and the news was nightly a lie, turn to nap her kohlrimmed eyes on this bedhead and muse to herself as if making a program inside her own head fair and uncarved, "What is that man in that forest thinking, is he thinking at all and what is going on with him that he's in the forest to begin with?"

But more often, dulled, she'd say dully to herself, "That is a man in the woods and that is all he is, that is a man in the forest and that is all he ever will be—he will never do any better!"

She'd say to herself, "He will never get out," as if she'd do any better, "like me he is stuck!"

She was herself like wood this daughter but like deadwood because she'd been chopped from the roots of her life and left unwatered to wither and die. She was hardened like bark (those were the stockings she stole from a friend), but absent mostly as if without sensation, which is to say that to men she was attractive because inaccessible in her emotions, her life passed her by like the jungle scenery in the background of Tokyo cartoons, her eyes glozing into knots and her mouth into a knot and her clear skin was in the mornings brittle but furrowed and rough in a wild way as if she'd been lasciviously dreaming and once a man—the building manager Blatnoy, a frustrated engineer who used to work in a warehouse but also on the side for extra money and goods fixed audio/visual equipment for the Politburo's connected (he connected *them*), he'd eventually become her husband spastic and fat in a camouflage vest its pockets bulging with tools—raped her not on that old wooden bed she'd inherited and used as a television sofa and outdated newspaper rack or on the newer metalframed bed in the bedroom she shared with her mother but instead in the kitchen where all political movements are birthed, him bending her over the plastictopped table then over the range, amid the greasy knobs she gripped as he left of himself inside her a puddle (but this had become a Kommunalka apartment, so rape went on while a lab chemist ate her cold supper in the hall, while the widowed librarian they were forced to take in last month accused in raucous tones the cosmetologist next door of toiletseat theft).

Her daughter that was made that day she gave birth to nine months later into 1989, not in their apartment—their apartment that was anyway no longer communal after her husband had managed to clear their cotenants out into other units in the building and, once they were finished being built, into neighboring towers newly irradiating from the dusty grassless central square of the complex—not on her old metal bed and not on her older wooden carved bed either where even a mother as late as her own had once given birth, but instead in the municipal hospital in a hospitalroom with three other mothers and one doctor collectively pushing, pushing more. A flat bland brown building, the hospital, with curling edges as if it were peeling—like a propaganda poster from the wall of the sky.

The daughter she gave birth to, though she resembled initially a wad of chewing gum, grew up—her ridges stretching into shapely arms and legs, the bubbles in her inflating further into impressive breasts. She was to be a person of more plastics and faster cars, of more freedom. She would live to enjoy the openness and transparency of fallen walls and no dictators with birthmarks in the shapes of tropical islands on their balding heads telling you anymore what dates and coal production facts you had to memorize at school, while, if you had the money, there was travel available to such tropical islands and any movie or book you wanted was yours if you wanted it and even if you didn't it could be yours still, you could have any food and drink at any restaurant or club because you could hold any job and start any business and could say whatever it was you wanted to say—"Fuck my elected representatives," "Empathy is Evil," "World War II never happened"—it no longer mattered in any sense of mattering.

But to her for whom communication was not a juicy long letter written invisibly in citrus or milk but instead a quick click on a keyboard, *Dear New York! Dearest Turkey!*—to her for whom free and openbordered choice was not a matter of allegiance or belief but instead a test of her appetite or depravity, for her the bed kept in the hall she used to sit on when she tied her shoes whenever she went out, the bed acting as bench under which she kept her shoes for them to sleep if they were tired, for her it was a bed and nothing else—in her childhood she'd hardly registered its existence, you would've had to have asked her, pointed it out to her and asked her about it—and the carvings on it were just that, carvings, it didn't matter what was depicted just that the thing itself was an antique, maybe, and did it have a value, could we sell it, where could we sell it and what kind of money could we get for it? For her the man there was a picture of a man and the woods there a picture of woods and the wood was wood with the value of wood and rather it was the value of the depictions that in her adolescence began to interest her—that a picture could have a value separate from that of its materials she was just becoming aware— when her mother by the year 2006 had gotten sick with a hardness and a rigidity like wood in her stomach and then in her breasts and regularly she had to go to the hospital again sunk in grass faded thick and long like the hair she lost and the weight and her color, this time not to give birth again, not to foal even her tumors, but only to die— Which brings us to the purpose of our story . . .

This story will not end as it began. No more trashy tellings like this, no more folktales. Here is a folktale that will end as a story, as a novel if we're lucky, but still nothing to compare to the audio/visual.

Better to just show the bed! Fairies! Better to roll around on the thing and hear it sing! O spirited sprites!

There once was a folktale, but its telling had been forgotten over the course of generations. One day, however, a story was written about a lost folktale. Does it seem that what had been lost is now found? or only, like bone chips and deer tracks, explained?

"Once upon a time there was a bed." And it was old and slept on as if sleeping itself down through the generations. And the generations generated because everyone married to have children and some of the children were born on the bed and some of the children only slept on the bed intentionally or not in the midst of watching television or listening to dance records or reading, God forbid, reading, and the children were always young but the bed kept getting older. It was falling apart at its seams, at its supporting beams, its boards would creak and give with loose joints, with loose joists, its nails snapping in two. And the parents of the children became grandparents and they too were *falling apart*— like beds themselves, sleepers fit for the coffin's lid with splintered limbs and the feeling of an ax pain brought down between chin and chest, termite infestation in the liver.

With her mother cancered in the hospital and dying, this daughter who's young and beautiful, this skinny gracile sylph nymph left alone for week three of chemotherapy invites over to the house the friend she'd met that evening at a popular pub whose theme was Dublin, "the friend" who doesn't speak her language and is from another country but still has many dealings with modeling "representatives" "representing" "many" "regional" "publications" and who before leaving his home in American Ohio maxedout a credit card on camera equipment, a light and a microphone to tape to it, which all he trundles up the steep stairs to her mother's apartment (her father, the engineer, had abandoned them both a while back under circumstances that even the most omniscient of narrators would blush at), hauling this gear with the help of his, "the friend's," local pardner, a parttime "event promoter" who also drives their van parked outside and alternates, in their movies, his penis.

When the foreigner had made her the offer at that fancily priced Dublin pub that evening, she'd offered to his pardner who spoke her language as his own, It might be fun? and the pardner agreed.

If I like it in life, why wouldn't I like it when we're filming?

No reason, no reason at all.

Not wanting to befoul her mother's bed—which she lately thinks of as her mother's sickbed where the woman lies usually so pierced with thermometers in every pit and fissure as to vomit their mercury into the nightstand's drawer—she leads her guests to the television's bed, that old wooden heirloom she insists on in a moment, a moment of dignity when "the friend" says, Fucking nice bed! I dig the carvings!

She sits down on the thing and he stands across from her an elasticized waistband's reach from her nose as they begin with their talking, the script they're scripting as they go along ignobly worthless and, I'm 16, no say you're 18,

I am 22 years old and say, "This is my first experience"—and suddenly, the rehearsal's spilling into the rehearsed as he holds her and presses his beery lips onto her he's taking off her clothing and putting his fingers into her and working around her clitoris with the knot of his thumb. Grk, grrk. Foreplay giving way to penetration as in he goes and out he goes and in, the noise from the bed overwhelming, its protestations offensively loud—her as amatory amateur and him as professional "friend," they're fucking the bed apart, the bed will be fucked apart. Grrk, grrhk, with each motion of their fuck being filmed by the pardner who stands across from them in the hallway on a chair pinched from the kitchen then up on the windowsill with a pointed shoe like a crowbar prying at the door—coming in close to zoom in, then going farther away again for a wide shot, and closer, and farther, and closer, and far, with each motion the sound of the dying bed overpowering any sounds they'd make, even any sounds that could be overdubbed by them or pretending others in vanside postproduction.

The bed wrecked in its throes, the noise of its legs and spine as if the chatter of the girl's rickety bones—an agony of creaks, a brutish splintering of howls and gurgles—them going back and forth and back as the pardner with the camera, lights, and sound, pulls in, pulls out, in again then zooms out on the fourhorned raging bed wobbling mortally, it has knees now, it's on all fours now as they fuck on all fours atop it, ripping out tufts of mattress hair and popping buttons like whitehead pimples and, though we never know her real name just her naked beauty (how when she's on top her tits turn dizzying circles, how when he doggies her her breasts hang down like lucent bunches of fruit, like lamped grapes the veins), though we never know her real name just what she'd told him her name was or what his pardner had told him, interpreting, when he'd asked her just like they'd rehearsed, "My name is Moc" (practice it, pronounce it *Mots*), she perhaps knows his name, because 12:46 in "the friend" shrieks—we can just barely make this out above the bedsounds—Say my name! Say my name, bitch!

But Moc the bitch does not respond, or can't (and only later does she speak again, garbling what she'd been told: "It tastes so big, it feels too sweet," i t.d.). Anyway the bed from their sawing atop it is too loud to hear whether she responds with his name or not—her mouth an unlanguaged vowel as he slams her once, pulls out, pulls her toward him again, a leg gives way, two legs give way and they're leaning against a hallwall and the wall's rughanging that's purple and gold and damp with sweat, with fluids his and hers in toecurled arabesques, and panting as he straddles the splintered wood and her and strokes himself off into her mouth and onto her face in splinters that are white and the trees are wet and white like in another season (the calendar in the background, tacked to the opposite wall, shows nature and says, in translation, *May*)—the trees, the trees, the trees are webbed with sperm.

II. Com/Moc

1. Com_____

They say in this Industry you need a professional name because then it's the professional who's guilty and not you, then the profession is at fault and not you or your parents, your schools or the way you were raised.

This professional name—and no, it can't be as rudimentary or flippant as "Professional Name"— becomes a sort of armor or shield, speaking in newer terms a version of what this Industry in its more responsible incarnations requires: protection, a prophylactic.

A condom, a condom for a name.

(Or else, consider it like you would an alias for the internet, an avatar that can investigate realms that you with your own name couldn't. A safer way of being yourself, by being someone else.)

And they say that one not particularly unique way of identifying this unique professional name is: first name the name of your childhood pet and secondly, as surname, the name of the street on which you grew up—in which case I'd be Sparkin West 2nd after my parents' dog (that shepherd we had for only a year, though I was also something of my doggie's dog), and a lane that subtly grids the wealthier suburbs of Jersey, where my father sits wrapped in the robe of his disused urban planning degree as the hypochondriacally retired founder of a successful addiction counseling business and from which my mother, trained as an historian, commutes daily to the city to edit the travel and health sections of a trendy magazine for women and men who read like girls.

Which is how I've come here or why.

From now on, in accordance with accepted journalistic practice, I will keep myself out of it. Kept distant, alone. He was no journalist but the son of a journalistic mother who in middle age had capitulated to exposés on waxing and superfoods that stop aging—and his assignment so vague as to be birthright.

Grow, change.

He'd heard different things, not from any pros who know but from hearsay, from wasteful reading around the internet, clicking through the links.

He'd heard that his professional name should be, first name the last name of his fifth grade mathematics teacher, de Vaca, last name the first name of his favorite aunt, Diana— and so de Vaca Diana. Or else that he should use the first name of his favorite brand of candy and as last name the full name of his favorite baseball player who played for the Giants until getting enmeshed in a major steroid scandal— Berry Berry Smackers Barry Bonds. That was what he'd do in school. He'd sit with notebooks, filling them with pen, with pencil, with names. Of other people he'd rather be, of other personalities. He'd sit with pen and pencil, gnawing their spans to match the gnarled branches just beyond the window, wet with rain, saliva. Always a thigh warm against the radiator. Then Ms. de Vaca, Mr. Heller (English), Mrs. Rae-Heller (social studies), would draw the shade.

He was a mediocre student, but in order never to work every degree had to be obtained.

College was enrolled on the other coast, expensively intentionally, though it was called a university, despite its being the only institution that accepted him.

It was May and all those not vicious enough to have found an offer to stay seaside went home to their agrestic Midwests, back to Mommy and Daddy, inferior internships, inferable jobs. And he was going back too, he was scrambling to pack the room into the U-Haul rented for the week—pick it up on one coast, drop it off with another franchise on the other.

He'd found a parkingspace too far from his door, down the block. Opposite the dogrun overrun that bright breezy Friday, the benches surrounding filled with profs and students who dressed like profs, standoffish admins lisping infidelities by phone and the hirsute homeless underliners of paperback books—he passed them sweating up and down the three flights from his room to the truck, down the block, each load he carried farther down. Weightlifters in the park, lifting weights, lifting weights, lifting weights in reps, in tight swimsuits, in reps. The busstop crowded with blondness for the beach. Hot and blandly still. Clear. That scape so different from this, so different from here. (But it seems this might be the incorrect approach.)

He laid the carpet down in the back, then the shelves and endtables and wobbly coffeetable and coffeemaker by the kitchen corner, above a low shelf kept always for his pan, his pot, his fork and knife, spatulation. He was drenched, wiping the hair from his face then stooping to lift, with the knees, with the knees, his body carrying the boxes and its boxy self—overdressed in sticky jeans, but all the shorts were packed—in sudden jerks, in spasms. Bicycles swirled around, walkers walked and runners jogged, a tanned xanthous man in the park, lifting weights, lifting. Everyone was light, was weightless, he felt, and only he was sulking, pale and big and bloatish, loading himself down in this lumbering truck—he'd become a mover, a slomover, a driver, a slodriver, he had no plans for what would happen at home or what he'd do with the degree he wasn't picking up. Media, PR. IT, finance. Generous options, given Mom's connections. This country should take only four, five days to drive—he and Mom were supposed to have their conversation come Friday next, graduation being that week too, he wasn't sure which day.

When he was finished clearing the room he sat on the bed wondering if he'd forgotten anything, but he'd only forgotten what he was sitting on—tedious, it couldn't not be overlooked—Ms. Zimmer's bed, the saggy loaner.

He scooped through his pockets, the jeans dried rough and hot, felt the truck keys, found the keys to the apartment. He left them on the pillow but didn't leave a note, no paper—he'd coordinated his departure with Ms. Zimmer's root canal appointment, giving dumb excuses about slots and fees, the traffic.

It'd been too soft a bed, it'd gone too softly on him, he smoothed it, smoothed the pillow too, he'd never had sex there, he'd stopped even having dreams.

He called his parents to say he was leaving—sure as he was that his mother wasn't home—left a message:

I'll be back soon, Dad, nothing special to eat, just make sure to make the sofa up downstairs.

He thought about just sending an email, then thought the better of it: he'd email them later, as reminder, forty-eight hours or so into his crosscountry drive—on a heartland signal wavering like grain in the wind, wavering then true, fixed and true.

What would he say then? what would be the Subject?

The man who invented email—sending messages from one computer to another—never revealed what was said in that first email ever sent. Unlike with the innovators of the telephone, whose testimony we have—unlike with the first man to swagger pithy on the moon.

What did that first email say? why did the inventor

never tell us? Probably because that message was obscene. Probably said, "Sveta, lover, I want to fuck your face off!" or, "Daddy, why'd you touch me there?"

This was Illinois.

He'd been up all night so late that it was two nights—so this was Illinois. And had finally slept by dawn and woke by noon, undressed at his computer.

As he stretched a yawn his computer woke too, its screen confirming: he'd bought a ticket for an international flight departing in six hours.

Such are the problems you get giddily into when you have access, the situations brought about by life's late convenience—how convenient it is to be connected, modern.

His parents' credit card.

He checked out of the motel—as if his purchase on bliss couldn't be roomed anymore—found his rental, that cumbrous truck packed fully, got behind the wheel, and drove toward Chicago—he was on the highway, he'd clung to the outskirts.

He left the truck in extended parking—one lot the same as another, or it's only that he's misplaced the number, his section, his row—there unburdening himself of his dirty bedding and dirty clothes, the corrugated boxes of incorrigible books, loose Registrar slips and Bursar receipts, the last days of being a student condoms optimistically purchased, bilingual dictionaries overdue, photographs of parents but none of friends, not that he wasn't into photography but that he had no friends. He had a wallet on his person, that abused credit card.

The check-in clerk asked, No luggage?

He said, No thank you, but the clerk didn't laugh, a mousy nondescript whose only pleasure was making hassle.

OK, description: her eyes were small and her vest was on too snug (he couldn't look at other women).

Then he explained, he had a girlfriend where he was going who had everything already: clean boxerbriefs his size, toothbrush and paste, multiflavored flosses—all he needed was his computer, computerbag on his shoulder.

Imagine that truck, then, the back of it.

Open it, scroll up the rear door and what you'll find is his room, wholly intact, packaged just as it was: carpet sample put down first, then the shelves surfeited with shelfware, the two lamps on the two endtables below the two speakers installed one each to the high rear corners, the interstate miles of stereo wire, even the empty bottles he wanted to keep as proof, the winebottles, the beerbottles—proof of what? 80 proof, 90 proof—he'd hung a couple of frames on the truckwalls for art: one abstract, one not, a print of a celebrated portrait but he always forget of whom (though "a muse," she had to have been).

Still, he couldn't have slept there, couldn't sleep even in the bedroom's original setting. Not that he'd neglected it, just that it wasn't his. Ms. Zimmer's bed, her spare, sitting back on the other coast in an otherwise stripped room, waiting for her sergeant son's disposal (after court, after a doubleshift policing Venice)—it'd been lying around her basement for years before she'd struggled it upstairs. She'd rented him the apartment, offering the bed only to rob him on utilities. He'd stolen the linens in revenge but then remembered they were his, he'd bought them, white on white. The mattress still pristine, the frame as unsturdy as it was the day he'd put it together again—decrepit, a pall plot missing screws.

Now his last communication, after passing through Security—not that phone message he'd left on his parents'

JOSHUA COHEN

machine, but the email he sent from this airport halfway across, the tarmac tailgating the plains.

Crosslegged by the gate, he wrote, he typed:

Dear Mom, I've gone on assignment. Reserve me space in the spring issue next year.

Dear Dad, Hope your disability case goes well with the Port Authority. I can't think of a second sentence for you.

Sincerely, David.

He pressed Send.

Your message has been sent.

His message has been sent.

XXX

He'd wanted a different life, a new life. Which should have been as easy as buying something. As simple as opening a new account. He'd wanted to make a new name for himself and the new password that would access his secrets would be ("preferably some combination of letters and digits")—no, no passwords. And no different names—no name at all.

Whole afternoons used to be as quiet as that Illinoisan motelroom was by dawn—once upon a time (childhood) whole weeks and even months passed by that satisfied, that ecstatically calmly, drugged on the horizonlessness of time, on his being alone and lazy and too young to know any better, before the days became broken up by access, noised by opportune technologies.

He'd been rockabyeing in a rockingchair, then on the bed, thickly rumpled. On that motel bed big and foreboding, as large as the room and as hard as the floor, a lump of carpet topped with a pillow as sharpcornered as a box. Through the window he saw the parkinglot, the truck, a smudge of moon, a muggy night, the window fogging. The bed was soundlessly elemental, like a boulder or tree grown up from the floor, from the fields, the soildark asphalt. The television could be turned on but no higher or lower than no volume on Channel 3—the remote control was missing.

He plucked an Apple—his. It had been a gift from his parents—for his birthday, for their having oblivioned his birthday—congratulating him on having been graduated from the age of being gifted. Whenever his parents gave him a gift it was so rarely specified what occasion it was for, often one gift would have to suffice for an entire year and then in one month, spring's, there would be this random, guilty superfluity of presents.

It was insufferable, their worming. His mother had deadlines and the internet (where she'd met her new friend, whose Manhattan condo she'd been staying at most weekends), his father had not having his mother and a phone that followed him everywhere (though only his addicts ever called and he didn't get out of the fridge much)—this was their remorse. His computer. Peel the screen away from the keys and all the letters glistened. It could spell *cultivar* and *calyx* and *stamen*, it could spell *exocarp* and *endocarp* and *mesocarp* and *pome*—it could spell *spelling* and *apple,* a-p-p-l-e, *apple*—all while circumscribing the cryptogeography of Eden, vegetarian recipes, porn.

The white box whirred as he began to waste—life the same as battery life, he couldn't be bothered to plug anything in, he was tired but wouldn't yet crash.

He had to sap the stress of driving—enough driving the trees and the roads, the rubbaged rumbling shoulders—this screen less boring than a windshield.

How could he even begin to map what was inside his

Apple, its pulp contents? its seeds? On top of everything, on the desktop, there's a folder called *Davids documents* and in the folder called *Davids documents* there's a subfolder called *Sophomore_year,* which contains in itself subsubfolders called *Math* and *Science* and *Math_again* and *Science2* and *Language-and-literature-requirements,* which contains inside not a folder anymore or folders within folders like a Slavic doll nested one doll within another within another like they're pregnant already—that's what happens whenever a user turns his back and leaves them, even toys, alone—but files, files upon files listed and named and the names of these files are *Gandhi* and *Gandhi-one-more-time* and *Pilgrimsprogress* and *Pilgrimsprogress-final* and, lastly (alphabetically), *What activitees I did on my summer vacation,* which is a file, no, an essay, no, a paper from as early as fifth grade, which begins: "What activitees I did on my summer vacation was to go with Mom to gazebo. We went sailing and I got 'severely sunburn,' the doctor said, then chickenpox also and laid in bed with vanilla ice cream, taking weird smelly baths . . . The End," he actually wrote, "The End."

He sat out on the furthest bough of his Apple—leaned against the cold headboard, plastic, against the cold wall, the wallpaper testing its pattern of bars. He was a file called *Him* in the folder known as *Motel*—the motel's proper name lodged in the throat. Its decor was worse, inconsequent. A mess of burns, of stains—but who hasn't read motel descriptions before? who hasn't stayed in motels themselves? Any description would be extracurricular unless he could blaze another way, an alternate route—the green road branching from the red road, the main road always the red road smoldering down south into the black.

Imagine there is a God. Just imagine, you don't have to all of a sudden believe in anything and cut your scrotum or go bathe your head in rivers. Imagine to yourself that there's this omniperfect entity looking down upon us all, with eyes, with real anthropomorphic eyes, really looking. Now, imagine He's doing so from just above this motelroom, which is a rectangle of sorts, it actually looks like a screen—and there is no roof, God has taken the roof off Himself. You can locate our hero in the lower righthand corner. There, he's a dot. A forgettable pixel, the whim of a bawdy baud. You thought only a splotch of coffee, a sneeze's stain or semen. But him, picture him. Now, God or the motel's invisible management, take Your giant finger and place it over him, Your cursor. Place it directly above his face. Directly above and blinking. Click.

He opened a window—not an actual window onto Creationdom, just something we call *a window*. An opening into a new otherness or alterity, not to make it sound any better than the depressing it was. Though it was good the motel got such good service—he was connected, stably online, for a fee. To be added to his bill. Spending so much money, so much of it not his.

He was tired of unfinishing delinquent assignments, tired of rereading homework done in a rush. He entered into the browser the address, which he wouldn't store in memory. Instead he'd stored it in his own memory and supplied it every time. Daily, often twice: www., the name of his preferred diversion, .com, which stands for "commerce"—he pressed Enter, depressed, also called Return.

This site he frequented on select evenings and weekends and weekday mornings and afternoons loaded new vids daily, that's how they'd advertised at first, "Tens of New Vids Daily," then it was "Dozens of New Vids Daily," and then in flusher times (flush the fraught tissue down the toilet), just "New Vids Daily Cum Check Them Out," and sometimes he sampled those new vids while at other times he sampled the other vids he'd missed on the days he'd fructified with only one or two of the tens and dozens on offer. An incentive to, as the site's top teaser banner advised, "Xxxplore." None too brilliant but comprehensive, the site gave variety, moreover, it was free, he assumed supported by its ads: swinger networks popping here, loading there the freshest fleshlight sextoy (now phthalate-free), longdistance callingcards (Centroamérica).

We wish to communicate how guileless he was—there in that middling motelroom as in his dormer apartment, no expert, no connoisseur. He had experience but no discernment, and anyone who tells you that the more time you spend with something the more particular you get about it has never been stuck in a marriage to his parents, has never grown up a boy with appetites and television: more is only more of more and to invoke subtlety or fuss is merely to show fear in the face of glut—Jersey boys in neon motels are never intimidated, they're never afraid.

They just drop their pants (he dropped his pants). Stretched the underwear down— there's no concern for not being prepared, no worry as to whether or not he's ready. The computer is always ready, the internet's always open (he's never been unattracted to himself).

Bound by gridded paper, between panel ceiling and patchy carpet, he was as erect as the walls, as hard as the walls (telling someone how hard you are is to flatter yourself in lieu of claiming girth or length).

We shouldn't be so crude. Though we're sure whatever document we've opened, still unnamed, still unsaved, we're sure it won't be saved. *They-say-in-this-Industry.* Keystroke, stroke. Drag to trash.

When you're on that first page or window of the site,

when you're in its Home, you're faced with a list of vids, and each vid is advertised, in a sense, by a still from the vid, a stilled scene from the moving scene to come—a freeze-frame or screengrab, a capture.

If you like the looks of that single, practically measure-less moment, you click on it and the still image loads into a moving image—the vid moves, *a movie* (we can't justify explaining this here, it just feels like it needs to be said— we'd rather not presume as to the depravity of our audience: Hello, Mom).

A taste is always given first, a still and silent taste, be-cause if everything was sounding and in motion all at once, all the vids, you couldn't decide which One would gratify desire, you'd become confused, Mom, and the warmth of your breath would become the overheating of anger.

Her screengrab seemed unpromising—he didn't know why he clicked, maybe because even in the context of ama-teur porn, theirs, hers, was the most amateurish and he felt for that, not erotically, he felt pity. Even in still silence it came off as wrong, as wrongly incompetent. Fuzzy, un-focused. Angled oddly. The fan whirred to cool the drive, cooed. His mouth was dry, tongue heavy. It was a corner of her mouth then a swatch of smaller penis (onscreen all penises are smaller), a tracery of drool.

The room was dark. Nothing existed outside the spot-light of the screen—bluish, greenish, mucoid, queasily regorging—nothing existed outside the weakly fluctuant cast of its halo.

How could we remember any of the vids before her? how could anyone? She erased them, what deleted them was her apparition, her apparency. Though we might, like the virtual does, lie: we might say it was a big lips blonde that did it for him, or a shy spinnerette with tiny thimble-plug anus, we could say Latina mature with redblue hair and puffy nips for knees, we could say young teen hairlessness, Black Mama, we could fabricate forever . . .

He was of a generation—no, bad word, bad habits . . . we're trying to say that everyone is our age now, even if they're not. We all grew up with this crap, we didn't know anything else—like Dad did, who masturbated to paper, to brownpaperwrapped magazines: pages glossy like lips, breasts shot verso, recto displaying recto, the navel that is the centerfold. Magazines not like the ones you work for, Mom—not fair that your son's father had to be your husband too (though Dad never mentioned sex).

Our generation doesn't have to hide anything under the bed, to secrete the forbidden in the closet, behind the shoes, behind the socks smelling like semen, the socks smelling like shoes. Instead ours is a practical pornography, with no awkward visits to newsstands or subscriptions to renew—there are no secrets, the entirety is acceptable. The computer sits proudly on the desk in plain day. There to help with the spreadsheets, with directions. We can just press a button and, naked lady. Press another button, another lady, nude. Point, click, penetration, it penetrates, it rewires your brain. You come to expect that all women take it up the pooper, take goop on their faces and into their mouths and, swallowing, that they all do so voluntarily, with nary a complaint in rooms like this one: unlived-in-looking, filthily-linened, plywood-doored.

You—

You are not always a reader, you are occasionally a human. You are, often enough, a human who is not masturbating. There are other things to do with your hands.

Write. Type, type.

Write, *I want to be a writer.*

Write, *I am a writer now.*

As a human, ask yourself—would you describe, publicly, losing your virginity? Would you, Mom, freely detail the first time you ever had sex in love or how exactly your husband or boyfriend moans, what they say during sex in the throes, would you tell that to a stranger, would you make report, could you bring yourself to recall and divulge that night you faltered or conceived, that sensation—and here we're asking Dad now—of being inside someone for the first time bare, unsheathed, how that felt so wet and hotly illicit without protection?

If you know how difficult that is, to describe such feelings and to do so unabashedly, without scruple, then you know how difficult it would be for us to describe this—this vid, her sex in it.

We will not describe it, we cannot—describe her hair, her dense brownblack hair and thickly furred furtive eyebrows of same, the brownblack but also yellowish eyes their flicking lids, sorry, we won't describe them either. We will not describe her interview—brief because ashamed of accent and, he suspected, a deceiver in her answers—cannot describe her undressing, how slow it was and how methodical her removal of clothing to bare skin like a cashier she was meticulously smoothing one item at a time, folding each garment like a bill at the edge of that fantastic bed we won't describe that gave such horrid creaks when she threw herself upon it flat and splayed for his ravage, apologies, it sounded like—*it sounded like*—

We won't narrate the foreplay, what of it there was, first kiss the last, the same as the last. Won't detail the oral, cannot in fact put into words the oral eyes that flickered in and out of contact. With him, with the camera. That first push into her, through her, stop. The jointed sighing, sighing. Won't describe the swirl of breasts like clapping hands, as he—the man—pushed in and out, in and out and in. The two positions requisite then the third—missionary, her atop, reverse cowgirl leveraged canine from behind—the old bed's collapsing rattle. Couldn't hear her voice. Couldn't hear his own. Won't describe the sound as *wrenching,* a car crash of woods and metals. Then him, "You like it you like it, what a pussy, say cum for me baby," and her, "Come for me baby, tastes too big, feels so salty"—two lines shot across the breasts we won't describe not even one, that dab on her tongue, collected in a dimple of her cheek.

The broken bed widelimbed, a dead huge hairball spider—we won't describe any of it.

That's the problem with the screen, you can't. You're always one step, but the crucial step, removed.

2. Moc

Hello my name is Moc and today I have make my first sex on camera. Just for you @ 1stsexoncamera.com

Let's try that again, he said, just read the card he's holding.

The card? she asked.

Read it.

Hello my name is Moc and today I make my first sex on camera. Just for you @ first-sexy-on-camera.com

Try it again.

Hello my name is Moc and today I make sex with cameras. Just for you @ first-sexy-cameras.com

Say it com, not *cum*—do you know what that means?

Hello my name is Moc.

Can you stop? I asked you a question. *Cum*—don't you know what that means?

Com?

Yes.

No.

Cum means open your mouth and take what I give you. *Cum* means open your fucking mouth and take it.

Fuck?

Good. Do you know what the redlight means?

Redlight?

It means fuck. Means fuck till I *cum*.

Fuck means *cum*?

Very good.

Money?

How much I say?

You said 5000 much.

That's what I said?

You said.

3000.

That was their exchange—and, *Cut!*—unfilmed. But later they'd pretend they'd just met each other, when they began filming, when the redlight lit red.

O fancy pantsing you here, what's your name, beautiful? do you want to go back to your house and get better—*ak-vaynt-ed* was their pronunciation?

ON, we're rolling . . .

Moe, "the friend," his pardner holding the camera—having dealt with the lights and mic—holding the cuecards too, because the girls could never be trusted to remember: Say the website's address at the beginning, repeat it at the end, www., with shotwad slopping from your face.

They were just passing through.

Who are you? the girls would ask him, would ask the pardner, Who is he?

He'd answer, I'm just passing through. Hanging out. Hanging. As if a gunslinger from a Western, a drifting private eye. Doing the circuit, the stations, making passes. The tiny villages off the highway. Little tiny townlets far enough from the capital's allures. He could've been a bonafide desperado, a bonded dick—none of these women, these girls, had met an American before.

Have you ever met an American before?

She shook her head, they shook her head into smoky curls, into corkscrews—Say, No.

And though it was the same script every time, each fall was as unique as its fallen:

In each Location—as they called every town where they porned—the first thing they'd do would be to identify the raggiest regional newspaper, where were sold birds not yet caught and deceased grandmothers' furniture and preowned cats, the paper most people used to wrap fish in, to wrap trapped Rodentia for placement outdoors and severed limbs too, in the hope of reattachment—their ideal a paper that informed on local gossip while providing annual photos of the mayor in a goofy folkloristic helmet slaying a marionette dragon at Carnivaltime, this being the news most preferred. With papers like that rates were cheap for double columns in inksmudged color and half or even full page spreads, but they always requested something small so as to seem special, unobtrusive—a small box relegated to the crossword's classifieds, a clue.

He and not his pardner, who'd always ask to place it himself, would place this advertisement and the ad would say: *We want girls 18 to 25. Must be nice.*

But it said all this in the wrong language, in this language—"the friend" didn't know the right language, he never would, the language things were in over here. That was the problem that was, at the same time, an asset—that he only knew how to speak what was not spoken too well by must be nice girls 18 to 25.

He was from—I don't know where he was from—Ohio, where his mother lived, say. He was big, broad and jangly in big fat stretched college sweats, always sweatshirts, always sweatpants (he didn't like zippers, he didn't like teeth). A whole wardrobe of that mottled blackswirled collegiate gray—a color that exists nowhere in nature. He was a beerdrinker with a beergut like he'd swallowed a keg but also swollen all around—beerwrists, beerneck, beerknees. Eight countries' worth of change in his pockets. He wore sandals, never socks.

Strange—I was always hearing about the no socks whenever I asked about his looks—his toes were long, his feet flat, apparently he was bowlegged.

But I've heard other things that conflict.

That despite being baggy—"skin like a paperbag," said one woman who introduced herself on a streetcorner on my first morning abroad, a girl he'd propositioned at a public pool—he was actually a trifle handsome. He was bald, not bald, balding, with black plastic glasses, with bluetinted metal sunglasses in the aviator style. Prescription, nonprescription. Never with a baseballcap, never without one, glasses resting on the brim, no glasses but a single studly earring. Hanging down from the cap a fringe of grayish white hair like an uneven row of incisors grown from the back of his head.

"The friend" always with a toothpick. "The friend" never with a toothpick. The ladies asking, Who is *toothpick?*

I've also invented a lot, for you, for myself.

After his mother remarried—a soybean farmer—he moved in with his ailing father: Sandusky, then a suburb of Indianapolis, and then New York for two years for film school. His father paid tuition, incidentals.

Imagine, two years of incidentals: Central Park swanboating through springtime afternoons into one night stands with women from the same hall, from adjacent dorms, with divorced faculty who'd loan him keys to Harlem—the next mornings the endless circling for an uncrowded bagel brunch, before a mile of museums to trudge, jamming to gentri-fi in Brooklyn, gentri-lo-fi in Queens, buying skank weed in Washington Square.

And his face was said to be a square, though wrung loose, spongy, and he didn't shave that often, he didn't have to—he shaved down there more than he ever shaved more north. When it came down to it, he wore no underwear so that his erection poked its hyperactive contour through the sweats. Jingling testicular pockets stuffed with coin. His cut cock was as hairless as a tongue. And had a tongue's dimensions when flaccid. When it came down to it, "the friend" had only one language fluently—this speech emerging slickly before the punctuating cash.

Whereas his girls had many languages among them: they spoke Slavics like Catholic Polish, irreligious Czech and Slovak, and Hungarian, which is not Slavic, and Orthodox Ukrainian and Russian, which are.

Moc—which was or is her name, whether it's a pornonym or not I didn't know then, I couldn't have—is a word common to all Slavic languages but with multiple meanings and in not two of those languages does it mean the same thing. In Czech, *moc* means "extremely," "very," or "much," and in Slovak *moc* means that too, but it also means (I've been told, I have no way to gauge for myself) "might," or "force," while in Polish *moc* means something like "might" as well, though I've been told it's more accurately "strength," or possibly "power."

How do I look? they'd ask unclothed, disrobed from solo showers, embedded.

Look good? and, Good, "the friend" would answer from atop her, or from behind the camera if he'd let Yury indulge, *Moc* good.

Men had used guns and fountainpens previously. They shot hot bullets into the mouth of the enemy or wrote vast scrolling poems to denounce their close friends—and this was how a life was destroyed. Several ounces of dun lead in the skull or *O your politics are as ideologically corrupt / as an autumn without pears.* And only memory would remain until the last remembrancer, he who squeezed the trigger or wrote the rhyme, had perished himself, his memory gone with him—but then they invented the camera and nothing would be forgotten again.

Moc was then—Describe yourself.

Use your fantasy, your imagination—your sister as model if sister you have.

As blackbrown hair with streaks of blonder dye like the markings of an insecure woodland pest runover by a van on a highway also striped like her hair, eyes bluewhite—but raptured with revelry's conjunctival bloom in the stills he took for his personal album, the tattered scrapbook "the friend" kept in the glovebox, along with the maps, Yury's ammunition—just a barrette over 5', converted from the metrics she gave, 105.821 lb. the same.

In her purse was an apple, at bottom the tobacco from a broken cigarette like a crushed finger.

And her phone, stored in it the last number she'd dialed or that had dialed her. ("The friend" kept boxes of new phones in the glovebox too—a new number sometimes each village, sometimes each trip.)

Her wiping up with a towel—having dumped the phone and apple from the purse to locate her lighter—was the last shot in her vid. A light for that comminute cig. Or to spark the mortal kindling around her.

But then the lens fluttered its lashes, blinked its cap—and she wasn't there, she wasn't only there:

Moc wasn't at home anymore, Moc was home already.

Whereas "the friend" lived in the capital. An expiscatory expat who'd recently sunk the bulk of his inheritance from his father's death back in Indiana (diabetes???) into a gorgeous old palace in the old city center. Wainscot for the halls, bespoke boiseries for the rooms, faux chambres set with arched fireplaces like windows—windows to flame, to hell—pastel friezes arched above the doorways depicting either nobles hunting a stag or a stag running away from a band of men intent on pinning it down, forcing it to admit what it really symbolized—Nature, innocence or freedom, art thou Christ?

The stag ran around and around the rooms, above the doors, insouciantly gallivanting mantels, gamboling sills, threatening to shatter the rosette and tulip moldings, the ceramic tiled stove. The parlor areas—there were perhaps three proper parlors plus two possible bedrooms he also referred to as parlors—he'd left flagrantly unfurnished: windy spaces canvassed with renovation's remnants, plastering arras, blank tapestries of polymer sheeting.

Even the Master Bedroom, the only bedroom occupied, was bereft—just a sleepingbag strewn small on the floor like a leaf fallen from a crude fresco of trees (eastern wall through northern wall continuous). The bathrooms were highly ceilinged—with a stock of mints in each bidet— the hallways long and, since he didn't use any of the un-reconstructed salons they connected to, utterly pointless. Only parquetry buffing the reflections of chandeliers— and of the screens on every surface: in the Master Bed, the Master Bath, suspended above the elevator doors, screens for screening, for televisionwatching and movies, screens for editing, for web support and maintenance, screens for power failures and backups (hooked to a somniloquent standby generator), screens for screens in banks.

The main entrance to all this flaunted an anteroom entirely empty except for a single tabling entity—a medium-sized chest or toppled armoire cluttered with par avion and torn aspirin packets—that he called the piano though it was, in truth, a harpsichord. He never played it but sat on its stool occasionally and when he looked at the stool and saw, instead, a steeringwheel, he knew it was to time to get moving.

He was hardly at this home, however, and so did most of his living, as he did most of his editing—his editable living—in transit. On the road. Always being driven by that swarthy pard with the spray of sesame seeds across his face—potentially a birth condition—and breath that smelled of "pomace" (according to the dictionary of one interviewee—an evenbanged brunette with diacritic zits who contacted your correspondent about a week after he landed in-country—who gave Yury's name as İlgiz İrekovich, said he was partially Tatar and the father of her child).

Barreling in that bloodred van (all the interview subjects mentioned that, as red as blood), from borders as illegible as signatures, to checkpoints blurry like their stamps. While idling at a crossing, the joke was: Where's the separate lane for the Americans? The guards kept the envelopes they were handed, sealed—they didn't need to be reminded of their lines.

From goatweed town to village, the farther away the better, the better chance at gullibility on the part, and it was a part played, of the girl. Same gist, different oblast. But never getting so far from civilization—twin crowhaired Gypsy subjects stated that Yury had told them—that they'd lose their signals: their phone reception, a dependable internet connection (who were the sources for the rest of this? bartenders and barbouncers and disco DJs, an incompetent candidate for a regional legislature, the owner of a settlement's only electronics outlet where Yury had bought brake fluid and nine volt batteries once, and, of course, obviously, local girls—girls who'd declined advances, girls with kasha teeth and bellies like pregnant dumplings who swore they'd refused "the friend," who promised they hadn't been refused *by him*—never a girl eventually filmed, never One who'd become a star).

Usually the morning after they'd met at whichever hamlet's lone bar or wannabe club he'd call her whose number he'd tattooed dramatically along an arm in the midst of frenzied dancing—he'd call early to disorient, waking the girl only to do her the favor of giving her an hour, for her parents to clear out for work, for her to apply razor, makeup, brush (he and Yury slept in the van or, if awake, "the friend" would flip through last night's polaroids).

They'd arrange an interview as if this were a professional engagement—*this was* a professional engagement—meeting for creamed coffees at the hamlet's sole barclub reopened by morning as a canteen serving what can now be confirmed as a light but succulent Frühstück (when "the friend" wanted to persuade through intelligence he'd find the German word).

There he might ask straight out to see some identification. The other conceit was inducement: he might neg and argue and feign incredulity, convincing the girl it was her idea to show it to him—figuring if she'd spread her wallet, she'd spread something else.

It was only when he saw her sum that he solicited (with allowances, reportedly, for girls whose age of consent was within a year or two or three).

After this vetting the appointment might adjourn to the van, its wheels astride the canteen's curb, where Yury, bleary, would buckle the girl up front and interpret the terms on the dash—explaining, or obscuring, the particulars involved, then guiding her hand to fondle the appropriate releases ("This is a translated contract, it says the same as it does in English," except it doesn't).

Though obviously an encounter like this was no guarantee, especially not when compared to an email—the prospects who'd responded to the ad, the pursued pursuing, seeking stigma with alingual typos.

That ad, being untranslated, flattered:

It said, If you can understand this you're special and deserve to be treated specially, you're the elect, lucky enough to give us an address and we'll drive up direct, hump our grip up eighteen flights of stairs to knock on your door (the elevators having been installed out of order)—you'll open and greet us, you'll hug us and kiss us, you've won us, we'll ply you with substance in thanks, then strip and fuck you for posterity—with your husbands and fathers and boyfriends out belaboring the docks and hangars, ensconced behind their paleotechnic computer terminals the size of motel-rooms, slobby in their pinching jeans and unironic tshirts, too tired to prevent or remedy.

You don't have to leave your tower, which was an identical copy of the prior tower visited, you don't have to leave your apartment, which was a perfect clone of the previous "flat"—a number of the females surveyed spoke a studious Anglo-English—you don't even have to be sober, shouldn't have to be sober again (the substances provided were vodochka, a nailbite of cocaine). If porn was concrete, these girls were cement—cement being the most important component of concrete, what makes concrete stick, what makes it bind, the rest is just sand, water, and air—without these girls, the porn would never adhere, the screens would go blank, the towers would crumble.

In winter, on a junket to a smaller burg whose snow and ice kept the populace indoors, "the friend" proposed to meet a girl vanside, parking that bloodbright mobile in the square by the townhall and plague column, by the manger and tree, by the monuments to horsebacked wars saddling generations with occupation. He drove the girl to her dacha—which was abandoned for the season—where they dressed a tripod in her clothes for a scarecrow, put a picnic blanket down and thawed the garden.

Another winter another dacha, but this dacha used year-round since the family had been evicted from their permanent residence for nonpayment. The girl's deaf or blind or both deaf and blind grandmother was exiled to the kitchen, while Mama—laid off from her banktelling shift, home from selling knitwear in the market—joined in her horny self—no need to look at *her ID*.

However, all prospectives were made aware: if there were ever any parental or supervisory issues that rendered filming in their cinderblock villa or cottage not feasible, or just undesirable, "the friend" was prepared to relocate to virtually any area cemetery, junkyard, or gully and fuck in the back bay of the sanguineous van—amid the hubby spare tires and jutting jack, the encompassing external drives and menagerie of woofers and tweeters—with always newly purchased, still in its shrink plastic bedding rolled down: latex beneath her, latex inside.

They'd make do with the van instead of renting a room or putting up at a pension—but was this because the accommodations available were so horrible (the bedbugs scuffling, hatched from the sconces)? or because when a room was cheap, its trouble was free? As policy, shakedown money, to neighborhood operators or the mafiavory, never was paid. Yury kept a gun in his pants, the uncircumcised coming more naturally than feminine circumspection. This amateurishness, a voluble amateurishness, was their aesthetic, all of theirs.

And finally—after the rubber was removed to unleash another manner of voluble across a girl's eyebrows—there'd be an outro Q & A, postmortem.

How much did you like it?

I liked it *moc!* very much!

Last session, "the friend" had mislaid the cards, and a

vibrating pouch of dildos and lube, and so here he'd had to improvise—with bottoms ripped from pizzaboxes scrawled across with marker:

"My name is YOUR NAME. Today I had my first sex on camera."

Say it, he said, waving the cardboard spotted with cheese-gobs and grease.

My name is YOUR NAME, today I—but this peroxidized little sister of a girl he'd had the previous Easter was interrupted by a drip in her eye.

Just for you @, "the friend" prompted, and the sister, who'd been sororally recommended, repeated.

Say, Goodbye.

That day might have seen this girl's first sex on camera, but not on film—nobody used film. Rather they used a format more indestructible, yet even more evanescent—Digital. "The friend's" digit dangled at its largest size, glabrousized. Then shrank at sixty frames per second.

After the redlight was no light, was dead light, it was his turn in the shower. He toweled his cock dry, put it to sleep in the cinch of a drawstring.

Yury was packed.

By the time our peroxider had gathered her halter and mini and arose—she'd ascended—upon her pleather stilettos, "the friend" had seeped through his pants.

So was she still named *Natasha?* or was she *Molly* [from] *Darabani,* as she was posted last week? or was she *Poly* [sic] *Sofia,* as the commentariat corrected? but what about this *Obsessa O'dessa*—is it me, or did I take ballet class with her?

Anyway, her name was never *Natasha*—she'd given "the friend" the name of a friend.

In their vignette, "the friend" called himself *Greg*.

Now *Natasha* did it for the rush, *Molly* out of desperation, and *Poly* liked the cash—but what about the girl who bore them all, gravid with their shame?

She did it for the hope.

These women lived in hope, they lived for the future as if they were every one of them already characters in a movie that projected well beyond one orgasm's duration—a movie of constant orgasm being constantly filmed: a wishful collectivist biopic accumulating footage—incessantly accumulating reels and gigabytes of footage—for all that dirty work of editing into coherence and happy endings somewhere years from now and countries away.

They lived as the aspiring stars of the movies of their own lives, which themselves contained the movies of others (much as nuclear reactors contain their cores):

Like the Innocent boy from around the block movie about an Innocent boy from around the block who begins driving a better sportscar and sporting better muscles, crucified in a black leather jacket, hung with gold chains (though he sold heroin substitute, though it was said he sold women—look how motivated he is, look how rich—*Innokenti, I remember when we both were just kids*).

Like the movie about the defense contractor billionaire who'd financed a production of his own out in northeastern Randomstan, but without even filming it, with epic thousands of extras but no cameras or crew: it'd been a Passion play, one night only staged on the steppe, ever since being nearly hazed to death as an Air Force mechanic he'd wanted to experience that many people taking orders from him— the one about the former bricklayer turned gas refinery tycoon who, to repent for having inflicted Orthodox baptism on his ten year old stepdaughter (and to mortar his relationship with her mother, a lingerie importer), had bought the girl her own television broadcast: she'd babble to the world about her friends, boys, school, and sport for an hour each night at eleven—the port concessions magnate who'd financed a judge's vanity recording of Liszt—the financial services mogul who'd commissioned a mural of his transgender mistress/master for a flank of his bank—the politician who'd hired a Muscovite screenwriter to ghostwrite a book exposing the corruption of his, the screenwriter's, uncle, a Navy embezzler who'd sunk submarines: the nephew took the work, he was broke.

This was an ambitious time and the girls knew their movies—they knew those had by hearsay or passed down the bulvar as well as they knew those of their siblings and intimates—they traded their stakes and plot points and narrative arcs—they quoted from them until they couldn't separate the quotes from their own conversation—they repeated and repeated them, you couldn't avoid them, you can't avoid summary—they even ambitiously invented them to reinvent themselves:

A man thrashed his wife whose head spurted oil—another billion, trillion—googillionaire. A man from the next town over, it was said, always just the next town, battered the gut of his pregnant wife and their son was born fluent in C++ and Chinese. Soon he had women at his door lining three deep, begging him to go to work on their issue. Then yet another nouveau oligarch who'd kickstarted his fortune marketing fire extinguishers throughout the Baltics or Balkans, parlaying that lode into funding lucrative eCommerce interests—it was said (apparently, it even made international headlines), he intended to launch a blue whale into space and was designing a shuttle whose fuselage would be equipped with a seawater tank. Once safely in orbit, the tank's hatch would open, releasing the water and whale to float dead forever in blackness—our earth a bruise the size of its eye . . .

But the most successful of these movies, the widest cited, it seemed—whenever a teacher assigned the composition theme of *Hope,* whenever any of the girls skipped their composition tutorials to hitchhike to the gorge for a swim only because they were young with plombir skin and fit and ruthless and happened to spot speeding from the opposite cardinality a vehicle as red as (some of these epithets were used, others are fictitious) "the Soviet flag," "a fire siren," "the covers of the Russian passport," "menarche"—was this, was the story of "Mary Mor."

Which is also the story of the unpopular Hollywood film *Sleepwaker V,* dir. Edison Lips, 1998.

Sleepwaker V is the most famous but also only film of this "Mary Mor," who does not star in it with her name shining pointedly above the title, but plays Hotty #3, whose total screentime is ≤ forty-five seconds.

"Hotty Mor" as she was called—with the accents of these tellings a binomial classification perhaps best transliterated as *Chotty Mor* or *Khoti Mor*—was a success story to trump all success stories, her movie widely heard of but seldom seen—it became more potent the longer it went unviewed, as if an ineffable dictator.

She was a model of what every girl wanted—not just an actress, was she a model too?

Her recent naturalization by the United States government revealed her to be Toyta Dzhakhmadkalova—and this attempted journalism, this inept investigative reporting, is dedicated to her.

She was born atop a tiny speck of static blown just outside Vedeno, Vedensky District, Chechnya, a mudspot like a mortifying stain on the dress of the land. Must be laundered, must be treadwashed by tanks. Russian was not her native language, she had no dialogue, she was frequently silent. Her home, an apartment complex hastily built to gird Vedeno's outskirts, has been almost totally destroyed. It was, by the time of her leaving, that proverbial heap of concrete surrounded by field the color of a suicidebombed circus and the miry consistency of mad tigress dung. The following things, things being weaknesses, made her cry: faded wallpaper in a scythe pattern similar to what they had in the kitchen of her family's apartment (but every family had similar wallpaper), last cigarettes not shared, dying ficus placed by unsunned windows (in apartments where none of the windows were sunned), cold tea—and now, for the uninitiated, the briefest of history lessons: border skirmishes by separatist guerrillas vs. Russians, Russian army incursions, hilariously vituperative decades of on again off again conflict you might've caught on television or not.

It has not been recorded—how Toyta found her way to Grozny (lit. *terrible*), capital of the Chechen Republic, following the First Chechen War. Perhaps she was there visiting a relative close or distant, the aunt of her aunt she called aunt too, the wife of a father's friend from hydroelectric engineering school she called Peacock—because of the woman's plumage, the feather she tied to her braid—but privately. Supposed to meet her at the bus terminal. Never knew which three o'clock train. Nor is it known how Toyta was supposed to have supported herself. Whether she cooked for monks or did laundry for a nearby madrassa, whether she cleaned floors for whatever government offices were left or washed windows in what official residences in the diplomatic quarter hadn't been razed. What retails as fact is that one night in an impromptu Grozny discotheque (formerly a dairy) she met a Russian soldier—cleancut, tightbodied, tightclothed in uniform plus mufti sneakers— who managed through bribing a general it must have been to bring her back to the site of his patriarchate: 180 kilometers outside Moscow and then, for a weekend, to Moscow Herself, neighborhood Ostankino, where a comrade soldier also discharged had an uncle who commanded a balcony over Zvyozdny (but the uncle spent whole months what was characterized as consulting in Crimea).

We will pause here to allow you to recite your PIN numbers to yourself.

By Saturday Night 1996, she'd escaped a Ciscaucasian death. Toyta would become, if the girls who'd tell this story were aware of the concept, *Immortal*—which Slavic languages too tend to render in the negative, as if it were regrettable: "never-dying," "never-ending." At a bar in Moscow she left her solider for a visiting American, a roving producer of pornographic movies.

This reporter was told that though the bar's ambiance blarneyed Irish, its name was very much of its place and time, ambitious, nearly excessively utopian: The Brothel Under the Sign of the Dice with Three Faces, Where Lesbians Drink Free on Sundays, Male Homosexuals Eat Free Every Second Monday, Where Behind One of the Toilet Tanks Is Said to be Hidden a Jew's Treasure, and the Rook's Nest in the Garderobe Has Been Formed from the World's Longest Lime Twig That if Ever Unraveled into Its Original Curvature Would Spell Out the Word *Typewriter* . . . (but I think here I might've been toyed with).

You ask, you might, how could an American who respects women and gives them jobs with equal wages and higher ed degrees and diligently keeps his paws off them— how could he ever expect with his solicitousness and always asking and nerves to take a woman away from a Russian soldier? from an officer—we've just promoted him—an officer with holstered sidearm, this major in Czarish bluegreens the color of a Romanov's blood? To answer that, however, you'd have to think bigger than masculinity, bigger than the sexpower of violence, of war. It should be understood that the American in the sideways porkpie hat still dangling its pricetag was no mere gap year visitor or sex tourist but an approximate Russian himself (such is the nature of the American problem: who are you? whose are you?), an émigré who'd come to the United States in 1984 or thereabouts via Israel and was here returned to Moscow—though he was born in St. Petersburg, or Leningrad, and had never been to Moscow before—recruiting talent or the eligibly cheap.

After Toyta had filmed a luxuriously uxorious—read: unremunerated—scene in his room in the starriest hotel in Moscow (don't believe it but this is what he almost certainly had her believe. with marble baths, marble sinks, marble floors, with beds as rare and expensive as arabescato and just as uncomfortable to stay the night in), this hyphenated-American, this Russian-Israeli-Floridian—Iosif, Yossele, let's call him Joe, regular Joe—procured for her a legitimate work visa #H1B and flew her to Los Angeles, whose airport bears the acronym LAX.

Los Angeles, despite belonging to dreams, also belongs to America. This means that Toyta's life was set, her survival assured by Marines. Here she could become someone named Tanya and this Tanya Someone could become a success. The rest, the dénouement as it's said in film, the finale, is scarcely as important.

In LA, Toyta/Tanya became Tina Toy, then, because she was once mercilessly lashed with the word "tiny" by a wheelchaired dominatrix in a Thai noodlerie's ladies' room, "your waist is soooo tiny!"—Tanya/Tina at the mirror slurping up the word in an endlessly looping waist of *tiny tiny tiny*—she became Tiny Toy, until a reputable casting agent she met at an audition for a low budget, character driven thriller told her she'd had her typed from name alone as black, not white and foreign—and so she became Mary Moor, who became Mary Mor (both at the suggestion of a Brit cameraman with bum knees who'd tried to date her), because in porn, which genre it seemed she'd be condemned to forever, there was already an established Mary More, another tanned to public transport upholstery texture girl with platinized tresses once notorious for the development of her kegels but now on her way out who, due to unspecified viruses—definitely herpes, allegedly hepatitides—could perform by industry decree only when protected, with the man maintaining on his erection a condom.

Toyta, for her part, was never infected with the worst of the diseases you could contract in America—doubt— she was positively immune to fear and doubt and so was incapable of being anything but fun, firm, and objectively reckless (not even that monthly test could scare her: the butch boss nurse, the kit's prick, a fink of blood to clog the vial—while waiting, she counted, the results always arriving punctually, by thirty).

It was on the set of a pornographic movie whose title has not survived and whose content has since like a failed family been broken up into short few minute clips all over the internet and there, meaning everywhere, aggregated under myriad descriptors and tags (the disparate keywords: *Teen— Interracial, Anal, Trib, POV, Mary Mor*), that she met a porno actor who—due to his 12" fame, the presumed prowess that went along with it, along with a concomitant legend regarding the size of the loads he routinely "unloaded"—was asked to play weekly poker with legitimate Hollywood television and film actors who only minced and otherwise faked the act of sex for much more money than was paid the people, just as attractive, who had sex really.

One Sunday during a game of Texas hold 'em, he ("Neo" of the prickly cactus muscles and tribal tatts, his head to toe entirely depilated) raved to his host's brother inlaw—this producer/director Edison—about his costar Mary—super*hott*—recommending her as a miscellaneous Eastern girl / stripper / prostitutka who might even be able to negotiate small speaking roles, ten words or less, tiny.

A boa slithered down a chairback. Edison's inlaw, an awardwinning screenwriter with an intellectual reputation, entirely intolerant of the career of his wife's kitschmacher brother, weekly invited the owner of a prominent Animal Handling company to play because the man, who worked only for topflight productions—dogs only for the best children's dogmovies, his lizards and apes regularly preferred over computer effects no matter how perfected—brought the snakes. A month before, and he could've lost his license for this, he'd brought a baby lion. "Leo" prowled around the balmy house, was soon forgotten and lost, only later did they find it stuck in the dryer.

The Animal Handler said this Sunday:

Them women from over there are gorgeous. But I don't know they worth the trouble.

He proceeded to tell the story of a friend and onetime employee (a janitor, a hoser) who had, he said, Ordered one of them from one of them services online—they sent her off and she ruined him, took every fucking follicle.

(The boa was coiled safely in a donut box.)

No fault divorce, he said, no shit, wasn't no time for fault. Four years in this country and the cunt was entitled to half.

Edison, shockhaired, sensitively chinned—before he produced he'd inherited his father's storage facilities throughout

LA, he'd joke on first dates that he'd inherited *emptiness*—told Neo to tell Toyta to come by the studio next Friday and—Hotty #3 was born. A minuscule part, a negligible role (Neo's bluff was called by a rash of queens, he'd left down $2K to Edison).

The film was the fifth in a series, a franchise—the fifth sequel, the pentaquel perhaps—but who recalled what the first four had been about, what'd happened in them when and where, who'd lived or died while making adolescent love on a rope bridge restive above a torrid ravine in Ventura steep enough to roll the credits down, there was no sense before there was no continuity . . .

. . . The old man, lupine, spry, and hairy, wiped down the bar and continued his story:

Unfortunately our Hotty's only line was cut, for being unintelligible. A tragedy—her words.

He paused, drank some sort of murky plumwater, took puffs on a short handrolled stub.

But then somebody uploaded that scene to the internet, he said, where to this day you can find it.

He turned behind the bar to wind the clock.

Business was changing, he said.

Movies where you sat in the dark with a hundred people groping one another gave way to television where you sat in the dark by yourself. Then the internet came around, cords became cordless, wires became wireless, suddenly entertainment was free and everyone's an amateur—amateurs at being themselves—because only celebrities are lucky enough to get paid just for being. Buy a camera, convince your bestlooking kinsfolk, upload, and Play—no more packaging, no more distribution where the smut's hauled out to the far bazaars among the bahns. This was democracy, this was enfranchisement, all that other sluttery you sold us—CocafuckingCola, shiny motorcycles parked between the legs of our mothers.

The bartender's eyes were elder, rheumy, his mouth disfigured, raggedly burnt and rimmed with moles like a castellated ashtray, like the hoops and arches of a crown. He snuffed his rollie, cleared the ashtray behind the bar.

His nose was a sharply tuned muzzle, was a hatchet. He was wolfish, vicious.

He said, Toyta returned to doing porn after her serious stint—she was savvy. She founded her own singlefee, multipass network—a dozen sites, a dozen girls, independents under her personal curation. An entrepreneura—that and not any implanted measurements is why her story is still told.

(I'm certainly polishing his English. Through the flit of whiskers he was facile but incorrect and interspersed locutions in French, in German, Italian—I've also filled in details and—no, you'll decide.)

It's said that the neighbor of her Grozny aunt had a daughter who was sold via Ukrainians to an au pairship in the West. My own—*Grossnichte, Grossnichte*—grandnieces, yes, grandnieces ended as Gulf commodities, whored to the oily emirates, the sheikh sex dens of Dubai—

XXX

He—I—sat listening to this story, to the script of this tale and to others. Dizzied by the dates and locales, the vertiginous names—what linguæ!

He sat on a stool at the bar and let this wizened bartender give him an education—this tender who'd taught himself the idiom by studying a UK travelguide "to Swiss." He had a cigarette and a drink, unidentifiable, he was learning how to smoke and how to drink, he'd been abroad for a month already but was not going back, he felt as if he'd graduated from even himself, that he was a new person now waiting only to receive the new skin to prove it—signed by no one, signifying nothing.

In the vid, behind Moc's head, a calendar had hung. The image on the page for the month of May showed a bouquet of blossoming trees—birch?/dogwood?/willow?—in front of the castle he'd stood in front of that morning (apparently, it was a renowned castle, though arduous to find—tired afterward he'd wandered into this bar at random, it had about it the rogue air of foreignness, of youth).

He'd had reprinted—at a kiosk in a webcafé huddled between a shashlik stand and a kvassarium—a stack of that screengrab, which froze mild May above Moc chastely clothed, or in that interim declothing phase (it was the only frame that satisfied all criteria): just her face and, regrettably, perhaps the top cleave of her breasts. He'd been asking around for weeks: Is this setting in any way familiar? do you recognize the girl or just last month? He'd handed one to this proprietor's hispid paw not an hour before—this proprietor who called himself Publicov and was closer to being an upright verbose lupus than anything human.

How do I know you're not another filmmaker? Publicov asked. Or maybe this Moc owes you money and you want to do worse things to her than what is done for the pleasuring of cameras?

He said to Publicov, You have to believe me—I was sent by her family in America.

Now she has family in America? The barwolf sucked his lips, fanged stiff the hair around them.

Cousins—I'm Moc's cousin from Jersey.

Roland Jersey—what did you say you were called?

Orlando, he said, Orlando Kirsch (first name the city his mother was born in, last name that of his father's orthodontist).

Publicov said, I don't know what I'm looking at, and lit another rollie.

Izvinitye, turning away from the smoke to busy with the bottles—containments undusted, displayed like women tall and smooth and without protuberance, ranks of uncomplicated women, easier to uncork, easier to pour.

But Publicov hadn't returned the printout, it lay like a rag sopping up the bar—the same printout posted that morning all over the ornate ironwork gates surrounding the calendared castle, on grave crucifixes in the dim midden yards of ruined churches, across the graffitied walls of gnomish humpy bunkers and imperious towers—glued and taped and stickered and tacked and nailed.

He asked Publicov, Please keep an eye out for her, telling him he was staying at a certain "Hotel Romantical," where he'd also left the desk clerk, an obliging pink boy of approximately his age, with a sheaf.

There was no text on this primitive poster save an address for an email account he'd opened the night of his arrival: meetingmoc@moc.com—the new address of his newest domain, $5/month in perpetuity it cost, and his bank, his parents' account at the bank, was scheduled to make the payment on the first of the month, the first of every month, and to do so indefinitely or until his parents' funds were depleted, which meant this empty website—*We're Under Construction, We're Still Under Construction*—and its full inbox of tipsters' emails might outlive him.

Publicov, finished prepping for lunch's rush, turned to

him and said as if in afterthought, And you might not want to try asking the police.

He said, So I won't.

We'll drink to that, and Publicov poured himself a glass, then refilled his, both to their brims. Together they clinked, took down the warm shots colored like a bruise. Publicov's glass hit a tooth, a slimy cuspid, which fell out and soaked in the dregs, a lonely rottenfaced fang. The bar was beginning to fill with customers, with noon, and Publicov must have been distracted. The drink tasted like the colors of the walls, like the turpentine that would remove that black. That spore, accreted grime.

The windows were open, the door, like a wing, aflutter. The crowd, on surrounding stools, in chairs at wheeltop tables, was vocal, was warming—they were sweating what they had drunk. Bluish ghosts wisped from their lungs but above him hovered only a miniature white cloud and he did not suspect his cigarette brand, he suspected himself, his soul (and hungered for a waitress—he wondered why there wasn't one around).

In a high nook, nested amid a thatching of cables, a television was playing sport—which sport he didn't recognize, he was too impaired. It wasn't darts—because that was being played against the door with a kitchen knife—nor was it a game exclusively of running or jumping. The rules, assuming there were any, involved a ball round like a spot but spotted itself, impregnated with a rambunctious demon, it hopped and skipped and jumped around as a team of perhaps fifty grown men had to run and avoid it, because it wanted to hit them and kill them, and the men could run but they could run only in the confines of the stadium, and the stadium, as the volume was lowered throughout the afternoon, got smaller and quieter until it was just a silent spit of light and he was alone with Publicov, who handed him his bill.

Dusk was just beginning, in the bar it was almost too dark to read—anyway the napkin had too many numbers.

He might have been drunk but still hadn't imbibed that much and said so and Publicov, offended, said, But it is only an address, maybe it will help.

Thank you, Publicov.

He thought, this book—this will be a book—is hereby respectfully dedicated to you.

He walked through the dusk to clear the head, to sober. Give himself time to decide whether to walk or be taken by what'd take him. The wind blew harshly, exhaled from the debauched cherubs' cheeks of the arcades. Lampposts lofted lamps that were out but the posts themselves were justification enough, drastic lancing efflorescences, metal trees set starkly against the grayscale of the sky. He decided on a taxi but couldn't find a taxi, could find no tram either, no tramstop though there were tracks over which to stumble, no buses or huffy marshrutky despite the poles that served as stops where he'd plastered over the timetables with posters of his Moc. Each cobble felt like a hill he had to ascend, a mountain, between them deep smutted river valleys filled with 50 ml nipbottles filled with the messages of wet butts. Pedestrians, mere bundles of cloths and threads and yarns, baskets with pasty arms and legs protruding and, from the tops, heads swollen like kerchiefed treats, passed him in the street, their very lives averted. Setts and pavingblocks gave way to a prospekt expansive enough for the parade of tanks and trucks in convoy, pulsing traffic away from the asbestine heart installed at the horizon—this city's entire historical centrum, intended only for the necrophiles and thanatos tourists, giving way to asphalt, the fancy fachwerk and gingerbread facades faded, even that fairy castle smogged, the leanings of centuries collapsed into piles of wood and stone until only boxes remained.

As if cardboard boxes, crates for the packing, stacked into towers, these hundreds or thousands of modular units making of the suburbs a boundless concatervation—as if the world had surrendered its rolling fields and city streets and instead cast itself up, straight up, as if the three dimensions of our experience had been upended, to two—as if he were headed toward not an address but a setting, a set . . .

How to explain such a scene to Sunday brunch readers at home? How to situate you—how to acquaint you but only with words?

Your correspondent did not know, your apprentice artist had not an inkle, how to describe the towering above him. Think not of livingspace, of cozy homes in distant faubourgs and kieze, but of officeparks, think of malls. Risen tiers and superseding levels of commerce, of store. But not stores as you might be used to them.

Where offices and shops should have been were domiciles, were private apartments—though from the outside, approaching the pathwork from the windblown street, they provided anything but privacy. They were glassed, they were entirely glassed floor to ceiling and any visitor could see in. He could look in where an accountancy should be and there was a family arguing at supper. Observe where managers should reign and surveil a grandfather at stool. Hello, grandfather! How are you feeling? how commoted are your bowels this evening?

A building cubicled, celled, seen—its exterior lit from within into a screen. The lobby door was locked, a smashed metal door loosely locked. He twisted the knob and pulled,

pulled. He checked the address again and the address was correct, unless a disgruntled resident had reaudited some numerals. Someone would leave, he was certain, he didn't know why he was certain—so vitrined, everyone appeared exhausted, appeared asleep.

He waited but no one came. He leaned against the jamb and, though he didn't know which unit he was looking for, tempted the buzzers, which were anyway unlabeled. He buzzed one and then another and yet another, but they were not buzzers. They didn't buzz an apartment with a familiar tone so that the party buzzed would be alerted that he was outside downstairs waiting for the door to open—instead they were eavesdroppers, they were monitors. When he pressed one he heard, through the fixture's grill, a baby's tin crying, when he pushed a second he overheard gerocomically gluttonous breath, fingering still a third, it was ragged sex, while from others was speakered indistinct talking, murmuration and scold, snoring, a lot of snoring and even silence, but needless to say only the silence baffled—perhaps that apartment was vacant or its buzzer, broken—and he didn't comprehend any conversation.

Moc—if she was in residence—which foursquare screen above him was her gleaming? which button would give him access to her sighs? In his hand, Publicov's napkin was streaking, had smirched—never having noted which floor was hers, it was presently expressive of even less: just a clot of phlegm, a florid spew. He considered hurling it like a rock at a pane—then went scrounging for a more stolid embodiment under a precise hedgerow welded to the ground—but there were no rocks and there was a redundance of panes. He threw the paper and away it flew. The swingset had no swings. The slide was a ladder up. The weather was as oppressively changeless as the consecution of the development's paths.

The door clicked and out staggered a group of intimidating children, overgrown children. Their youths were stuffed like sausages into the casings of overalls, in the fashion of gastarbeiters, their faces were slabs of borodinbread swabbed with butter, their noses whole potatoes and ears, the toothpicked rinds, their fingers livid burns as from carelessness with methpipes. They stared at him, spoke cacophonic codes and then—nudging one of their race forward, a manboy with crusty, distended lips, trollishly stunted—inquisitioned:

Does David ever make it back home—or, *Ever go home do David?* or, *Did home ever David make go?* and though through the measured, mechanical accent he understood the words because they were in his language, he didn't know what they meant until, a breath, he realized they referred not to him, rather to an American television show he'd never watched but had heard of—a hysterical serial, he thought, impossible not to have heard of (though it'd been over for a season, its antics supplanted), as he told this insistent, scarcarved, tough as warts horde:

Yes, David goes back home to marry Samara from college—though his father dies or is kidnapped for ransom, but only after his mother's investment firm fails or is arsoned, I hesitate to say which, and no—he said in answer to the youngest trollnik stroking his leg—no, I don't know what happened to your sister!

They lured him into the tower talking as if talk would be enough to resist them—them grasping at every scrap, at jeanpocket and jacketflap, at the frayed bills filched from his pockets and at coins—down a hallway suffused with noxious stench: fuming nettles, as if in the production of a remedy for this hallucination in progress.

The back of the tower was not, like its frontage, glassed, but concrete poured floors above a courtyard. Only the front's sheer veneer was new.

It was a courtyard strung across with links for laundry—light frilly cirri of negligee and peignoir, lowhanging nimbi of thong and garter—filled with receptacles and trash. And he was tossed like a bag of trash himself—thrown atop the bags, rolled over their blackly bodied putrescence, needle shards of mirror, a slough of diapered spoiled lard—tumbling into another hall, to his knees at the threshold of an opposite tower.

The boys emerged from behind—having slipped past the dumpsters at the yard's periphery—dragged him to his feet, to an entryway as dark as fur.

Just inside, seated in a chair with a singular daintiness, was a bear. A bear distinctly untaxidermical. It was a cross-dressing bear, if animals can be said to be transvestite, if creatures have enough gender identity to make their wearing of the opposite sex's human clothing something approaching a meaningful statement, any statement at all. A pince-nezed male shebear in a windsocklooking bonnet speckled with sunflowers, above skirts of billowing hospitalgowns patched with flag, the vex of a nation he could not place. The entirety had been cashiered from a fable, discharged from a land of porridgecomplexioned dwarves (his youthful escort, assembling protectively around).

The mamabear gestured him to a chair of his own, of a similar make: a fussy interiorism high of haunch, tiny of limb—as if not a perch but perched itself, upon fluted legs, the feet with chiseled toenails, with claws—upholstered in pelage, in uncomfortable quills that rustled with every shift and he shifted, he couldn't force himself to keep still. Between the chairs was a table as swarmed as the sexagenary square of a chessboard, draped with a drab spiderweb lace doily, set with a corroded samovar fixtured with a bulb, its stray filament illuminating two saucers, two companion cups. A battered phrasebook's pages folded down. Not a phrasebook but his passport, atop his wallet, blueblack both. And the keys to a faraway home tenanted, it must've been, by faraway and worried parents.

It was the dusty sittingroom of a pensioner with no children or none who visited regularly, only the relict thievelets who, kissing their mamabear's jeweled paw, raised that dust in the rowdy muster of departure. They shut the door behind them—that door set flush with the shadows—spun its lock, as if adjusting a radio, or as a vault is sealed—suddenly, it was as if he wasn't sitting in a room anymore but amid night itself.

He felt tickling, below it all—but how had he not noticed—a rug of bearskin.

His host growled in response to this inspection, said, Publicov's no liar—he said he'd never met anyone who wants a girl like you do.

So what type do you want, my dear? of what species, my dearest? I have every model in stock.

Slav slave or Central Asian combination? vagina where the anus is or anus where the vagina is? there's nothing we don't do: oral exclusive, mutual masturbation, S&M, gruppengrope, frottage.

I want one, he said, her name is Moc.

Roleplay then?

No role, Moc.

No doubt we have her too—with this, the bear madame growled a woman from out of the fuscation: a big brutish wench with a figure like a log her employer could hibernate inside, who looped her wildweed hair and pouted lechy her smacked black lip, where she had a sore.

That's not her.

Of course it's her—the newest version. You won't recognize the difference.

I want Moc.

You would.

The woman's giant trunking mass dulled abruptly into furniment again: secretaire, escritoire—into nothing that refined, just a handleless lunk of domesticated linden. Where you'd keep a will you'd like to lose.

And I want immortality, said Madame bear, but I can't have it—I want to own a helicopter and a yacht and a gym franchise, I want to downsize half my staff and fix the lottery in Kyiv—but who can live from wishes?

Who?

Having held every other bodypart, his hands could hold his hands.

Madame bear sniffed, said, OK, so you're searching for this Moc—I'll tell you what, I'll help you, I'll tell you how to find Her.

And from now on, dearest Reader, it's too late to doubt—

There is, the bear said, a place.

Then it covered itself with a shawl, tugged from a puddle in its lap—the fringe of that rug of bearskin, omnivorously soiled, full of thistle.

It was deeper night and eurous gusts found the spaces between words to fill them with their chill.

This isn't a story, David, *this is a place* (and here another creature's prose is indiscriminately enhanced: the bear's original locutions being even more melodramatic, more foreboding, stalled by tedious epistolaries)—but it is Far far away, it is dangerously enchanted.

The bear paused to siphon tea for two from the samovar looming like a fervid moon above them. Lighting his wallet, lighting his keys.

The brew was black and ropy, with a hint of citrus, of bergamot, then, he sipped again—it was still too hot—this taste unplaced, hot and dull but rublesucking sour.

He put his cup back on the saucer, placed the saucer atop his passport for a coaster: his passport picture, he felt, already out of date—it was mortifying and he hoped the bear wouldn't ask to examine it, wouldn't comment.

Or it both exists and doesn't exist, the bear went on, I myself don't know how it manages that, but you will.

My lovely, my darling.

Though when you'd know is precisely when you'd no longer be able to tell me.

It's distant, David, I can tell you that, then once there, go higher.

Go high atop a mountain, a hill that's been fortified, a walled settlement walled deep in the past.

At least you'd think it was centuries ago—all that mud, that woodstirred mud. Before electricity even—this is important—before all that current that connects the world like lines of latitude, reception like lines of longitude, the equator of constant signal.

The houses look that old too, they look ancient, they're falling down, their foundations rotted stumps, sinking, sunk, their roofs are thatched and leaking weather.

There in the center of town, because it is a town, there in the center of the center as if the hub where all the wheel-spokes meet, is a square, and in the center of that square is a well and if you gaze and gaze and gaze into that well late at midnight you will see, it's said, your own reflection—this is because there's a measure of water at the bottom—what else would you expect to see down there, tell me?

But.

(The bear tugged tight its holeworn shawl—that thorny fluff indistinguishable from its fur—then crossed one leg over another like a popular child psychologist, and this struck him as faintly ridiculous: one claw resting on a claw of the chair—the bear was smaller than he'd thought, it didn't reach the floor.)

But the inhabitants of this town—they are why it's so special, David, Orlando, friendly Greg—whatever you wish to be called.

Cinching its socky bonnet, the bear's ears skewed out the sides: mangled ears, one lively, the other limp, like the rushing minute and lagged hour hands of a clock.

When a girl like Moc decides to shed her coy lycras and molt her cloying denims to engage in sexual intercourse on camera, that's when it happens—that's when the, shall we say, "funniness" happens.

(Please forgive my language—when you recall in your own words how I've told this tale to you tonight I hope you'll have me speaking better.)

This is a special change I refer to, a sort of conversion. After they're shot, if you'll follow my explanation, after these girls are shot, they cease to exist.

Rather I'm speaking of an existence that's not an existence—after these girls are filmed doing what it is they do, they no longer belong to themselves but to the world, as they're no longer merely physical but image too, they are everywhere, they are everyone's.

Where do they exist then, ask yourself, *if they do?*

In themselves, in their own skin, or as imagined—as unimagined—on the screen in your lap?

They become women/nonwomen—having been used, having been overused, and so weakened, weak, there's a grain and a haze to them, a sapping depletion (indeed, everyone's fate is the same and is sordid).

Not anymore pure people of skeletonized flesh, yet also not purely data transmission of image and sound, they dwell instead in the middle—limboed, in an interim stage—abiding a gaplife as something between.

At best as an essence of what they once were—half theirs and half yours now: David's, Orlando's, gregarious Gregory and Yury's—shut into this secret repository, into this archive they live in, a cache of the senselessly undead.

For steadiness he sipped at his now tepid bitter tea, keeping his eyes on the rude snout of his ursal host, on the ear that kept twitchily ticking.

Your Moc—the bear producing a rumpelskin paper from a slit in its parachute housedress, the printout showing the Missing caged on a page, caged in a screen, depicting the Wanted at the very beginning of mid-act—your Moc is not as she was, but she is still herself.

She has already entered that other realm, that porousness beyond borders, that Freedom . . .

The bear crumpled a corner of the printout in its paw, dipped it in its own tea (untouched), began eating it wet. Those eyes nailing themselves into his. As drops of the drink smeared its fur, matting the fur that was just then wrapping around him, he who couldn't help but stare—at that lewd dewy snout, that lurid ear tick, the sharpened nails of those eyes—couldn't help but close his own now, he was exhausted, he was softly enfolded, he apologized, mumbling, he hadn't properly slept in over a month . . .

XXX

(notes for a videographer)

He wakes in the forest. It is dark and it is thick, with green and brown like the swirl of a clogged toilet. Wastepaper hanging from the trees, lots of trees. Sweaty profferings of verd as if not grown but enlusted, bouquets of let loose bush. Pubescent stalks sprung up between pawprints, deep but shallowly filled, like wells with toes, with talons, their moisture stagnant, a dankness pervades, the stalks decompose. Evidence of uprootings. Trees big and wet—when did it rain? up on their roots exposed like rusted struts, like scaffold. Hills just ahead like steppingstones to hills, like stones topped with walls of trees, with a sky of trees screening out the sun. (I'm doing my best here. This would all sound so much better in an original.)

Af yge enneb inle mezre ygu . . . it feels "like being inside wood" (as if I'd been spellbound, trapped, imprisoned within a tree, then axed). He's bruised all over his body, bruises brackish in color like his skin's a passport cover, or as if his insides have been stamped with the splotch of poisonous berries—apparitions smeared across his stomach, faces null like navels. Everything hurts, his ribs hurt. His arms and legs feel shorter, he feels smaller, like a boy, younger than a boy.

Wondering, wondering—what miracle decoction was that? what potion that stranger bruin conked me out with?

He's cold, wearing less clothes than he had been. Less a jacket, there's nothing returned to his pockets, there's no wallet, no return tix or pass. No oily key hard alongside his hardness, his wakingtime erection. An eye is swollen, a lip bleeds, he feels like he's broken a bone in his cheek. In his throat. He is thirsty—he goes.

The trickle is from a nearby stream whose water could not be anything but fresh, flowing, as even he's aware, from uphill even sweeter.

He follows, follows the stream's sharp dark carving of the hill, pausing only to wash himself and sip at a knotted pond, continuing.

This compulsion to ignore the fakeries and secondlives, for the origin, the source—he wants not the trickled down, he wants the wellspring only.

He trails through the woods, along the weedy banks in squeaking sneakers. The grain grades steeply, while the pits he has to avoid on his way are not wells to other worlds but the wet sucking prints of the outsize dogs that roam here. The big shaggy shepherding monstrosities he could ride atop—they prowl patrol around the summit's settlement, chaining the moat, the wall's circumsomnia.

Now he is hot, being so close to the sun—a lamp brought close by an invisible hand from above, swiftknuckled, silent. The summit rising only to flatten toward a desk, a desk-top. And somewhere farfaraway—the sound of pages being turned or the clicking of keys—a chair unreclining, brought closer, closer.

Each of his bruises pulsates, pounds, giving off heat of its own, like he has circuits secreted inside, like overwork has ruined them.

The dogs he recognizes, just then, he recognizes as Sparkins—a litter of them, more, litters' clones of the one he'd had to be named after, nicknamed after, that one disastrous year before his parents were forced to sell it, or maybe, he'd suspected, put it down, because Dad in his couched craziness got allergic. But Sparkins a bit larger than the Sparkin he'd had, quite a bit larger, even from a distance. Enormous lumbering Sparkins trundling their guard, stepping over stumps, stepping through trunkhoarded piles of leafy cereal flakes, flecked with crystals of sugar, of salt. Blown piles up to the moat, then on the moat's other marge up to the fortress wall, blown spoons and bowls and the smothering plastic that bagged them—as if cumulus that'd been slammed by the wind into the trees and wall, becoming stilled, dispersed, disincarnated.

This city, being walled, is inherently attractive—not just in the artificial picturesque sense. When you are not wanted in, you want in, but maybe making you want in is the sense of a wall, its purpose. Where you are not needed you run to make yourself, you must, indispensable. He comes unheard and unseen, but perhaps the Sparkins are used to him already. Unheard because of their enlarged dogtags jingling in stride, jingling like bells. Unseen because he sneaks his way low and nimble. Toward the bridge's access, the bridge over the moat. The moat heaped with gray and creamcolored boxes. With monitors and drives, modems and printers— all the elements of an obsolete technology, too useless to be recycled as another's access and so, their discard to hazard a fall: no water but a bog of coaxial cables in barbed coils, sharded screens of bridgelike wires, their innards exposed to spears and spikes, gutted lengths unwound to a murderous serration.

No foreigner storming invasion but a hero lost from

a bedtime telling of immemorial nights, wandered from a page: he stands as if a pixel, a lone pix fixed at the drawbridge's lip—a drawbridge, a moat, each flattened, flat, smooth the page, Reload.

To enter through the portcullis withdrawing, through its portal . . . (this is where I write from now—Dear Mom, cc: The End—I must have fainted).

I wake in a square, undressed but tended. My bruising beginning to subside. And in its stead, a glow fanning through me, as if the opening rose of health, as if vigor.

The town is a setting of lithic streets and alleys, the houses themselves logged of dilapidated wood—but lived in, not neglected, textured.

Nobody is around—no presences I sense directly—but I feel, I prickle as I feel—these floatings, these passings.

A brush of hair or a gusting sway, as if the skirt of the wind blowing by me, blushing up my cheeks. A skin's prick to horripilate the wrist, a nail's graze or a lovemark left by teeth. As I begin—this is how I begin—gradually, after days, a week, *to see.*

Everywhere—as if enclosed, as if my life's been flattened up against the seething surface of my eye—everywhere I look soon there are women, *there are girls.*

I see them, by seeing through them. Their beings projected onto every surface, on every ceiling and floor and sky, projecting across every window and alley's curve, across and as every doorway's gracious waist—the walls, visible through them in wrinkle crack and cellulite chip, in spall and score and peeling paint, temporarily aging them in their revenance. But then they float again, they pass again— eidola of posturing plank, with glints of screwy smiles— their youth preserved only in their motion.

Girls throughout alight and nude, or not nude but purified, thoroughly pristinated as I proceed—through the statics of climate—to recognize: Natashka one and another from that vid with the Cuban I think and yet another from a schoolyard seduction and still another from the bucked back of a moving truck and a girl I recall her name too, I think Masha, Sasha, Svetlana (trans. *luminance*)—and they are themselves but aren't, as they were both onscreen and you have to guess in life itself, but not.

You can speak to them but there's no indication, Mom, that they can hear you and certainly they can't speak to me, Mom, not yet—if they did then in what language?

You go to touch and you touch right through them. Snug a breast and end up feeling up a boulder, flick a lip and end rubbing tongue against a sill.

They just hover, Mom, amongst their daily tasks—gathering water they won't drink, steaming suppers they cannot eat, but I can.

I am sustained, they take good care, don't worry.

I've even stopped asking after Moc.

I'm sure, one day, I'll notice her appearance. As a shadow's missing features. As faced light thrown across a wall that is not home's.

Your message has been sent.

My message has been sent.

Links

Emission
abajournal.com/news/article/paralegal_sues_over_herpes_
web_post/

McDonald's
mcdonalds.com/us/en/food.html

The College Borough
pdfhost.focus.nps.gov/docs/NHLS/Text/79001603.pdf

Sent
iafd.com/person.rme/perfid=RRosenberg/gender=m/
Robert-Rosenberg.htm

Joshua Cohen was born in 1980 in New Jersey. He is the author of five previous books, including *Cadenza for the Schneidermann Violin Concerto*, *A Heaven of Others*, and *Witz*. His nonfiction has appeared in *Bookforum*, the *Forward*, *Harper's Magazine*, the *New York Times*, and other publications He lives in New York City.

Book design by Ann Sudmeier. Composition by BookMobile Design and Publishing Services, Minneapolis, Minnesota. Manufactured by Versa Press on acid-free 30 percent post-consumer wastepaper.